JUST DESSERTS

DESSERTS

A Novellelah

CARL REINER

ISBN-10: 1-59777-627-0
ISBN-13: 978-1-59777-627-1
Library of Congress Cataloging-In-Publication Data Available

Book Design by Sonia Fiore

Printed in the United States of America

Phoenix Books, Inc.
9465 Wilshire Boulevard, Suite 840
Beverly Hills, CA 90212

10 9 8 7 6 5 4 3 2 1

CHAPTER 1

Armed with the modest success of his last novel and the not too ego-damaging reviews, Nat Noland, feeling an urge to create a new work, typed *Untitled* atop the page and stared at it hopefully.

"Nattie-boy," he addressed himself, "this time why don't we take on something serious?"

"We took on Genesis last time out—that was pretty darn serious," he replied, answering his own question.

"I was thinking *weird*-serious like the rapture books those two religious nuts wrote. That left-behind series sold millions."

"Hey, let's do one where no one gets left behind," he added excitedly. "Everybody *stays* behind…by choice!"

"Yeah, and instead of going to heaven, they have a rapturously fun time on earth laughing and partying until they die, of natural causes, in their late nineties."

"…or early hundreds…."

"...while having sex!..."

"And we call it, *Going to Glory with a Smile on Your Face—and God's Blessing!*" he added, laughing.

"Perfect title...funny, dirty *and* spiritual! Hey, I think we've got it!"

"We've got enough. Start typing, Nattie-boy!"

Nat leaned back and thought about the creative conversation he had just had with himself. He was no longer self-conscious about engaging himself in audible discussions, and he had Dr. Frucht to thank. He thought now of his psychiatrist's parting words:

"Mr. Noland, you have managed to write fine books by talking to yourself, and I think you should continue this way. I see no reason to break up a winning team. You are, obviously, your best collaborator!"

"Okay, collaborator," Nat sighed, "start collaborating. Any ideas?"

Nat thought for a moment, then mumbled, "Let me try staring at my eyelids!"

"Yeah, that did jump-start one of our novels."

When Nat was about to start on his third book he had closed his eyes and concentrated on the back of his eyelids. While staring at them he saw the word "normal" appear.

"What *is* normal?" he had asked himself. In answering that question, the novel *Normal* was born.

So, once again, Nat closed his eyes, concentrated on the back of his lids, and within a phantom blink of an eye, the word "blurbs" popped up. He thought for a moment, then furiously typed a short paragraph.

"This is great!" he laughed, as he read aloud:

> *"At last, the novel we have been waiting for Nat Noland to write—a serious, spiritual and suspenseful work. If it takes you more than one sitting to finish this serio-comic peach of a book, get yourself checked for dyslexia." —Larry Gelbart, creator of the Emmy Award–winning TV series M*A*S*H and winner of Humanitas award, 2007.*

"That is original! A celebrity quote for a novel that hasn't been written! Our publisher is going to love this! More, more!"

"How about," Nat said, as he typed:

> *"In his new novel, Nat Noland once again demonstrates his ability to turn the prosaic into pith and the mundane into magic."*

"Pith into magic! I like that," he laughed. "Who wrote that?"

"How about Philip Roth?"

"Pith sounds like Mel Brooks!" he said, typing:

> —*Mel Brooks, author of Broadway's smash-hit musicals* The Producers *and* Young Frankenstein.

"Here's what Philip Roth wrote," he said, typing away:

> *"This imaginative new work of fiction could well be the blueprint for the brave new world for which we have yearned, and now know how to build. Bravo, Mr. Noland!"*

"Hey, instead of Philip Roth, make that Richard Dawkins, author of *The God Delusion.* I like having God on our back cover. God is hot."

"Philip Roth gave us a short, sweet one," Nat said as he typed:

> *"I hope Mr. Noland is planning a* Blurbs II.*"*

"Hey, what about getting these guys' permission? They may sue."

"I hope they do! Being sued by Gelbart, Brooks, Roth, and Dawkins is great publicity," Nat laughed, replacing *Untitled* with *"Blurbs,* a new novel by Nat Noland!"

"I like *Blurbs*," he hesitated, "but does it have to be a novel? It took over a year to write the last one."

"Almost two…how about a novella?"

"Hmm, a novella has to be at least a hundred pages."

"What's shorter than a novella?"

"Hey, remember how our shrimpy friend Paul Bluett's Jewish grandma called him Paulelah?" Nat said, laughing. "How about, '*Blurbs, a new novellelah by Nat Noland*?'"

"Seventy pages long!"

"A *pithy* novellelah could be *sixty*."

"Then pithy it'll be!" he said, typing "novellelah" on the title page. "Now, we can use an idea."

Nat repeated the words "an idea" half a dozen times before blurting out, "That atheist thing we started…! What did we file it under?"

"Under its title, which was a good one—*God Help Me Help You!*"

He was suddenly excited to bring up a file he had always intended to revisit. He had started the book with a letter to the Almighty but was discouraged when his publisher, Ross Davidoff, suggested that the title and the idea "stunk!" Nat tried not to think of the publisher's critique as he reread his letter to God:

Dear God,

I am a lifelong atheist who, of late, has been leaning toward agnosticism and secretly wishing that You do exist. In the off chance that You do, I would like You to consider a list of Ten Suggestions that I have compiled, which if you chose to implement would guarantee a world where all would live out their lives in peace, love and harmony, free of cruelty and man-made disasters.

This would come to pass if all human beings, while they live, can know and experience what their rewards are for doing good deeds and what their punishments would be for committing evil ones. Knowing that one's acts will bring either immediate pleasure or pain must encourage all to behave morally—and thus ensure a Heaven-on-Earth.

Almighty One, if this too be Your desire, as I must believe it is, then I trust that when You consider my list of Ten Suggestions, or as I call them, Just Desserts, You will find them worthy of divine attention and implementation.

As You are all-knowing and all-seeing, I assume that You are already aware of my list of suggestions, but if You are not, please give me a sign, and I will make the list known to You. I await Your sign.

Very sincerely,
Nat Noland

"Not too shabby," Nat said proudly. "Hey, when referring to God, I've capitalized the *G* in *God* and also the *Y*'s in *You* and *Your*. It looks strange. Wonder what God prefers?"

"I'll ask him when I see him," he quipped, "but about our list of ten suggestions—"

"Three suggestions! So far we've only come up with three."

"So, we work up a few more. Let's see what we have here. It seems we didn't write any of the rewards for good deeds, but here are a couple of the punishments for bad ones." Nat read:

> *The following punishments will be meted out immediately upon the perpetration of the offense!*
>
> *For Minor Incivilities. (A detailed list of incivilities to come.) One: A moment after the offense, the offender will lose his ability to walk and will instead...*

"Nat, darling," a sweet voice on the intercom asked, "what are you doing?"

"Oh, nothing much," he joked, "just working on a spiritual blueprint for building a brave new world."

"Well, stop for a minute and get the plunger. The powder-room toilet is stopped up."

"Glennie, can I take care of it later?"

"No! The Bluetts are due at seven."

"For dinner?" Nat winced. "Darn, I forgot! I'll be right there!"

Nat turned off his computer, retrieved his plumber's helper and muttered, "First, fix the toilet—then, the world."

CHAPTER 2

Ordinarily Nat looked forward to an evening with the Bluetts. Paul Bluett wrote the informative syndicated column "Think About This," and his wife and he were considered by all to be the perfect couple. They were the same age, the same height, had similar names (Paul Bluett, Paula Prueitt), similar senses of humor, and both were semi-recovered alcoholics. Three months after Glennie arranged for them to meet, Paula became Mrs. Paula Prueitt Bluett.

The evening was pleasant enough. Glennie cooked one of her signature meals, coq au vin, but the dinner conversation was less spirited than usual.

"Nat, your reputation as a host is at stake," Paul mocked. "My wine glass has not been serviced since the salad course."

"Oh, sorry," Nat said, picking up a half-empty bottle of Pinot Noir, "I thought you were trying to cut down."

"*Down*—not out!" Paul explained, holding out his glass.

"You must forgive Nat," Glennie apologized, "He's pregnant with novel."

"Oh, how wonderful!" Paula gushed. "Tell us about it."

"Yes, do, but first, act the proper host, pour!" Paul ordered, tapping his glass.

"So, you are off the wagon...," Nat commented, filling Paul's glass.

"No, I am *on* the wagon—the *wine* wagon!" Paul said, taking a sip. "Now, tell us what is furrowing your brow."

"You don't want to know," Nat grimaced.

"Tell me anyway...maybe I can help de-frown you. What's your book about?"

"Well, so far, I really have nothing."

"Nothing?" Glennie interrupted. "Paul, my husband is writing a, uh-blueprint...spiritual blueprint for building a brave new world—that is *not* nothing, darling!"

"It is...unless I figure out where it's going. At the moment, it's just a notion," Nat argued weakly, "and a pretty far-out one."

"What do you call it?" Paul asked.

"*Blurbs*."

"What's it about?" Paul goaded. "Maybe I can get a column out of it. Is this *Blurbs* a novel?"

"Well, it's a sort of novel...I call it a..."

Concerned that his friend might be hurt, Nat hesitated before telling him why he was calling his book a novellelah. Paul *was* hurt but also found it funny and somewhat flattering.

Nat, in turn, was hurt that Paul said he found the idea for *Blurbs* "fascinating." *Fascinating* was the word Nat often used when being kind to a friend's inept literary effort. Paul's comment might have discouraged Nat from resurrecting his old project had he not added, "Boy, Nat, do I envy you!"

"Oh, you do not!" Nat said, hoping Paul would elaborate.

"No, I really do," Paul insisted, patting him on the shoulder, "You have put yourself out there. I admire your guts!"

"Is this you or the wine talking?" Nat semi-joked.

"Both, but it's me who can't wait to see how your novel-lala develops."

"Neither can I...and it's a novellelah," Nat corrected. "Or maybe I'll make it a novel-lala if novel-lalas are shorter. Whatever it is, it's a puzzler."

"I love puzzles. If you need a brain to pick, mine's available."

"Is it available for lunch tomorrow at the Bistro?"

"You buying?"

"I'm buying!"

"Then pick away!" Paul said, emptying his glass. "The Bistro at one? I can sober up by then, but one-thirty is safer."

"Then, one-thirty it is!"

CHAPTER 3

To be ready for a productive lunch date with Paul, Nat eschewed sleep that night and spent it at his computer, defining his theory of Just Desserts and the punitive terms of his three suggestions to God.

JUST DESSERTS

SUGGESTION #1
FOR INCIVILITIES
(ANTI-SOCIAL BEHAVIOR)

THE PUNISHMENT:
Offender's ability to walk normally will be suspended for a length of time commensurate with the nature of the uncivil act.

SUGGESTION #2
FOR INHUMAN BEHAVIOR BY AN ADULT TO A CHILD

THE PUNISHMENT:
Boils will break out on the offender's person and remain until offender rehabilitates himself.

SUGGESTION #3
FOR LIES THAT NEGATIVELY
IMPACT OTHERS

THE PUNISHMENT:
The offender's punishment will be
dictated by the number of human
beings he causes to suffer and the
degree of their pain and suffering.

To make Paul aware of what they would be discussing at lunch, Nat e-mailed him the three suggestions for Just Desserts along with the personal letter he had written to God. Nat always smiled when typing Paul's e-mail address, BluettPrueittKnewit@aol.com. With his cursor poised to send the material, a devilish thought occurred to him and, for no apparent reason, at least one he could never explain, Nat added a second e-mail address: GodGod@godhelpmehelpyou.now. "Now that is an impressive address!" he thought.

"And it would be even more impressive," he said, as he tapped SEND, "if GodGod, etc. received my e-mail!"

Nat stared at the screen, dumbstruck.

"It went through," he muttered, "…both e-mails went through! It's not possible…*not* possible!"

"Yes, not possible, but," he argued, "obviously not *im*possible! Some nut-burger with a God complex or delusions of grandeur invented the same silly e-mail address I did."

"What are the odds of that happening?"

"Nine hundred billion to one," he said, ready to respond, "but maybe *I'm* the one!"

"Dear GodGod," Nat typed, giving his new pal a nickname, "What did you think of my ideas?"

Within seconds, two new messages arrived. Spooked by the rapid response, he inhaled deeply before reading the first one, which read: "Provocative ideas!" Nat was flattered that somebody, whoever it was, thought his ideas provocative, but on reading the second e-mail, he started to hyperventilate. It read:

"Nat, respect is denoted by attitude and behavior, not by capitalization. So, to answer your question…"

Fearing to read on, Nat shut his eyes and mumbled, "'Nat,' he called me 'Nat'…how did he know my name?"

"And how did he know I was thinking about capitalization?"

Nat's need to know if the sender actually used the word 'capitalization' compelled him to open one eye and peek at the message.

"When using nouns or pronouns in referring to me," Nat read, "notice that I did not capitalize the 'm' in *me*, nor would I capitalize the 'h' in *he* or *him* or the 'y' in *you* or *your*, or the 'a' in *almighty* or the 'g' in *god*. I know you did when e-mailing me. Most people do but that does not make it correct.—R.K."

"Hey, R.K., who are you?" a shaken Nat yelled at his screen. "I did not ask *you* that question! Or anyone!... I asked myself, and only my wife could have overheard me—and not even she unless I was talking out loud!"

Nat was seldom aware whether he was thinking or speaking his thoughts but, at this moment, he knew he was screaming them at his computer, and it was making him dizzy. By gulping down a half-liter of Fiji water, he managed to keep himself from passing out.

"This R.K.... This e-mailer with delusions of grandeur," Nat thought, "couldn't possibly know my name or what I was thinking or saying in my office, unless somebody bugged it, or if he eavesdropped on my intercom."

"Or unless this guy," Nat conjectured, desperately trying to comprehend the incomprehensible, "this GodGod or this R.K., who I think has delusions of grandeur, does *not* have delusions of grandeur but has...*actual* grandeur!"

Fearful of continuing to harbor this unnerving thought, a thoroughly confused man left his computer and walked, wobbly, up the stairs.

"Too weird, too weird, too goddamned weird," he muttered, then shouted, *"Goddamned weird with a capital G!"*

CHAPTER 4

Ordinarily Nat would go to great lengths to avoid waking his wife, but tonight he was so anxious to explain why he was shaking like a leaf that he jostled the bed rudely and grunted loudly as he crawled in beside her. She greeted him with a poke in the ribs and a request to "Shush!"

"You'll wake the girls," she whispered, then opened her eyes and asked dreamily, "Where have you been...and why are you trembling?"

"Because I just e-mailed God, and He e-mailed me back! Glennie, you're not going to believe this—nobody will, but I e-mailed God my list of Suggestions, the ones I was working on for that book..."

"Which book, darling?"

"It doesn't matter! What I'm trying to tell you..."

What Nat was trying to tell his wife, and did with jack-hammer speed, were all the incredible things that had happened to him in the last few hours. A very sleepy Glennie, trying hard to appear interested, offered a few "hmmms" and other assorted sounds that indicated comprehension. When Nat finally wound down, saying, "...and then He wrote that my ideas were provocative, and I have no idea what He meant by that.... "

"So, ask him in the morning.... Go to sleep," she said, rolling over.

Knowing he would toss all night until he learned what this R.K. meant by saying the ideas were provocative, Nat raced back to his computer, which now showed one unread message. He relaxed when he saw that it was from Paul:

> *i read yr material. my sobering brain*
> *had crazy idea—will chat tmorrow.*

"Oh, Paulelah," Nat thought, "your brain is going to need a drink when it hears whom *I've* been chatting with."

Nat typed GodGod's e-mail address and asked: "What did you mean when you said, 'ideas provocative'?"

Almost immediately, Nat received: "*You will know!*"

Nat then typed, "How will I know?" and sent it.

A split second later, Nat had his reply. It was the same message but set in bolder, more elegant type.

"Nattie boy, I cannot handle this alone," he said to himself, printing out the message.

"Share this with someone," he advised himself as he stood up, "Someone who can tell me I am not insane. If Glennie can't, she can call Doctor Frucht and have him tell me I am not going crazy!"

"Wake up, Glennie," he ordered, holding GodGod's printout in his trembling hand, "Wake up and look at this!"

When she did neither, he shook her.

"Honey, I'm sorry," he apologized, holding the paper an inch from her face, "but you have to see this!"

Peeking past her half-closed lids, she focused on the words, *You Will Know*.

"What will I know?" she whispered, hoarsely. "What is this?"

"My e-mail from God! I started to tell you about it...."

"Oh? Oh, yes," she recalled, "You e-mailed God, and he e-mailed you back. I thought I dreamt that."

"You didn't!" he shouted, "Remember that letter to God I wrote for my book, *God Help Me Help You*? Well, I e-mailed it to Paul and to a nutty e-mail address that I made up. *An address I made up!*" Nat yelled, slapping his forehead, "And I got this message back from that fake address! It's crazy—too crazy...and I don't know what to think about it!"

"Think about calming down, dear," she said, simply. "Now, Nat, you really don't think God sent you this message, do you?"

"I never think God sends me or anybody messages! I'm an atheist, frchrissakes!"

"I...I never heard you say that!"

"C'mon, Glennie, you've heard me say I'm an atheist hundreds of times."

"Yes, but never 'frchrissakes.' That is so not you."

"Did I say 'frchrissakes'? I did, didn't I?" Nat said, sitting down on the bed. "Oh my, something really strange is going on."

"Nat, you're flushed," she said, feeling his forehead. "Do you have a fever?"

"Oh, I hope so," he said, retying a shoelace. "It would explain these hallucinations."

"Darling, you are not hallucinating. There are dozens of logical explanations."

"Give me one!" he challenged, "Just one!"

"It might be," she said, getting out of bed, "as simple as you and this person, coincidentally, making up the same e-mail address...by the way, what is it?"

"GodGod@godhelpmehelpyou.now! What are the odds of two people coming up with that?"

"Even if it's nine-hundred-billion to one," she said, humoring him, "it could happen."

"How did you come up with those odds?" he asked in disbelief.

"Oh, come on," she said, putting on her robe, "You always quote those odds when you exaggerate."

"I know, I know," he said, slipping into bed. "See how off-kilter I am?"

"I see you going to bed with your clothes on. You're not planning to sleep that way…. "

"Who isn't?" he said, adjusting the covers. "I've got to be ready. There's a lot of weirdness going on."

"No question about that," Glennie agreed, heading for the bathroom. "You might want to work all this into…what are you calling your book?"

"*Blurbs*," Nat said, watching his wife disappear into the bathroom.

"You can use all this unexplained stuff in *Blurbs*…it could be a part of that spiritual blueprint you mentioned. Darling, you rest," she shouted, turning on the shower. "I'll get the girls up. Will you be lunching with Paul?"

"Oh, yes!" he said, "One-thirty at the Bistro…wake me!"

"With a kiss!" she shouted, stepping under the shower.

A drowsy Nat scanned his fancy-lettered e-mail, *You Will Know*, and muttered, "What, what... *what* will I know?"

Once or twice in his lifetime, Nat had wondered if he was going mad, but this morning he did not wonder...he knew. If only he did not have to wait until afternoon to do a show-and-tell for Paul. He thought of his three brothers and wished he could do a show-and-tell for them *and* their wives *and* for everyone he knew or ever met. Hopefully, one of them would have a worldly explanation for the otherworldly events that were engulfing him.

In spite of being awake for nineteen emotionally charged hours, a debilitated Nat was aware of his vulnerability. Sensing that he could easily collapse and die if he did not get some sleep, he ordered his mind to conjure up images of his darling four-year-old twin daughters. He pictured Greta and Grace asleep in their beds and willed himself to emulate them. He mumbled drowsily, "Have to go sleepy-bye...have to stay alive for them...have to write...be...productive...."

On the back of his fluttering eyelids, he saw bundles of money and on his computer screen—a thin book—his book...

"Blurbselah," he muttered, his eyelids fluttering. "Must write...pithy book...and pithy blurbs," he gurgled. "Nolan's 'new novellalalalalah' pithiessst ever...ten pages long...Larrry Glebharmdt... NewYawkTimesellah...."

And then, blissfully, Nat fell into a deep, coma-like sleep.

CHAPTER 5

Glennie thought that if her discombobulated husband were awakened by the angelic voices of their twin daughters, he might more quickly "combobulate." Thinking "combobulate," a word Nat invented, made her smile. The girls, who were snuggled on either side of Daddy, took a cue from their mother and sang:

> *When the red, red robin comes bob,*
> *bob bobbin' along, along.*
> *There'll be no more sobbin' when he*
> *starts throbbin' his old sweet song,*
> *Wake up, wake up, you sleepy head,*
> *Get up, get up, get out of bed!*

And it worked! Daddy's eyes popped open on the phrase "Wake up, you sleepy head," and with a smile on his face, he joined his daughters, singing a full chorus in almost perfect three-part harmony. Looking at their bright, beautiful faces made Nat feel that the world was back on its axis. The phone ringing, and Paul Bluett asking if their "brain-picking" lunch was still on, brought Nat back to reality and his tentative hold on it.

In trying to buoy his spirits, he thought, "I have not lost my mind, I have merely misplaced it," and jotted the phrase down for possible use in *Blurbs*.

For the hour and a half before meeting Paul Bluett, Nat managed to locate a portion of his misplaced mind and attempted to approximate normality. To awaken his sleep-deprived body, he took his normal five-minute shower, drank his normal mug-full of hot Postum and leisurely dressed himself in his most normal outfit—gray slacks, blue blazer and a white, open-collared shirt. What was abnormal was his distracted state. During his ministrations he imagined hearing a low-decibel hum coming from an unknown source. Initially, it did not worry him. He expected that the hum was inside his head, spawned by a stress-filled night, but he became concerned when the volume increased.

"Glennie," he asked, too casually, "do you hear a hum?"

"A hum?" she asked, brushing her daughters' hair. "What kind of hum?"

"It's not a regular-type hum," he said, cocking his ear. "More of a low, wavering hum. Listen!"

"Girls, be quiet for a moment," she ordered, straining to hear.

"Don't you hear that, Glennie?"

"I do! Oh my goodness, it's the freezer. I forgot to shut the door," she said, shepherding the girls out. "Would you shut it?"

"Will do."

"Thank you, dear."

"No, *thank you!* Nat shouted after her, "I thought it was in my head. I don't need another unexplainable in my life."

Nat was relieved that his sanity was relatively intact and pleased to note that the sound of the humming became louder as he approached the freezer.

"Hmm," he said, "never heard the freezer hum before."

"Some astute writer you are," he scolded. "How come you never noticed that?"

"Because freezers don't hum, that's how come!" he replied, slamming the freezer shut and opening the abutting basement door.

"And neither do computers," he shouted down to where the humming emanated from.

"There is no humming in computers!" he instructed as he descended to his office, then quickly

realized that the persistent humming was not coming
from the computer but from an image on its screen!
It was of a huge pink bunny hopping about and
humming a song, to which Nat now belted out the lyrics:

> *Hippity-hop bunny, hippity-hop bunny,*
> *You're a funny bunny, hippity-hop bunny,*
> *Hippity-hop bunny!*

For two full choruses, Nat happily sang along
with the hippity-hopping bunny, all the while
worrying how and why the song and the bunny got
on his screen.

"I'm guessing," he said, looking heavenward,
"that this is your doing."

He had guessed correctly, for when he
scrolled down he found three fancy-type letters, *I & P.*

"What the hell is 'I T P'?" he asked, then
realized, "It's not 'I *T* P.' The 'T' in the middle is a
fancy ampersand…it's 'I & P'!"

"Right, it's that biblical-type font," he said,
typing the fancy *&,* then the &.

"Oh, great, but what the hell does 'I & P'
mean, shmucko?"

"Ask the shmucko who sent it."

Nat asked, and the answer that was ping-
ponged back was the frustratingly familiar "*You
Will Know!*"

"*What?* What will I know, you sonofabitch?" Nat yelled, slapping the top of his defenseless computer.

"Take a deep breath, Nattie!" he warned himself, "before you explode."

"Any ideas how I can defuse me?"

"Well," he said softly, dialing Paul's number, "maybe I'll just talk this out with someone calmer and more objective."

Nat was hoping to move their lunch date from one-thirty to immediately, but Paula informed him that her husband was meeting with his editor, though she said he would be at the Bistro "on time or probably fifteen minutes early."

"Fifteen minutes early?" Nat repeated nervously. "Then, I will arrive there fifteen minutes early…that way neither of us will have to wait for the other."

Sensitive to Nat's unease, Paula asked, "Are you all right, Nat?"

"I am fine," he answered hopefully. "I am just fine!"

To prove to himself that he really was "just fine," Nat shut down his computer, strode purposefully from his house to his car, back to his house to retrieve his keys, then back to his car and off to lunch.

CHAPTER 6

Nat arrived at the Bistro a half hour early and fortunately found his table available, and on it a basketful of breadsticks. No matter how many cheddar-flavored breadsticks he consumed, he could not temper the anxiety and disappointment he felt when at one-twenty-seven he realized that Paul, who had not arrived fifteen minutes early, would also not be on time. As his cell phone rang, he bit angrily into a breadstick.

"Damn it," he muttered, intuiting that it was Paul calling to say he would be late.

"Hi, I've just started on my ninth breadstick, where are you?" Nat asked, chewing noisily. "Are you on your way? Hello!...Paul?...Paul? Who is this?"

Nat listened for a moment, trying to understand what was being said and who was saying it. It was Paul! A hyper, hysterical, unintelligible, blathering Paul who seemed to be speaking in tongues.

"Paul, for God sakes, slow down! Talk slower!" Nat demanded. "Paul, I can't understand a word you're saying. Paul, what are trying to tell me? Whoa, whoa...calm down!"

Paul could not calm down. What he was desperately trying to do, and failing completely, was describe something unusual that had happened to him a few minutes earlier.

A few minutes earlier...

Paul Bluett, always eager to participate in anything that might be fodder for his column, was anxious to be on time for his appointment with Nat. To this end, he cut short a meeting with his editor, dashed out of the building and commandeered a taxi that an elderly couple had just hailed. As Paul slipped into the back seat and instructed the driver to take him to the Bistro, a blinding shaft of the whitest-white light flashed from the sky and enveloped the taxi. It shimmered for a few seconds before it faded.

"What the hell was that?" a panicked Paul asked the driver.

"Yeah, what the hell *was* that?" the equally panicked driver shot back.

When it appeared that no damage had been done, Paul breathed a sigh of relief, which he immediately followed with an air-sucking gasp of terror. Without reason or warning, the two back doors of the cab flew open. Paul's body went limp as an invisible force lifted him from his seat, slid him out of the cab and rudely dropped him into the gutter.

The gathering crowd, who had watched Paul's magical teleportation in stunned silence, let out a collective shriek when the white light shone down again, and the mysterious force returned to gather up the elderly couple and place them gently in the back seat of the taxi.

The grateful couple, with smiles frozen on their wrinkled faces, waved to acknowledge the round of applause the crowd tendered them as the cab drove off.

Sitting in the gutter, a bewildered Paul could feel the eyes of the disapproving crowd staring at him. He arose sheepishly and attempted to walk back into the building, but instead of walking, he involuntarily did something that amused the crowd and terrified him. It took great physical effort to stop from making a fool of himself.

"What the hell just happened to me?" a panic-stricken Paul wondered.

His mind flashed to the e-mail he had received from Nat this morning, and the words "ability to walk normally." He had not understood it but recalled the phrases; "offender's walking privileges suspended," and "uncivil act."

"Offender? Uncivil act?" he asked himself, "Am I an offender? Whom did I offend? My editor? And 'uncivil act'? What act? My cutting our meeting short? This is madness, it's beyond madness! There has to be some medical explanation," he decided, "... like a muscle spasm or a neurological thing.... "

For a fleeting moment he blamed it on the amount of wine he had consumed the night before, then wondered if it were possible that the madness was attributable to Nat's spurious suggestions to God...and God acting on them? He scoffed at the thought that God, if he indeed existed, would implement Nat's stupid suggestions.

To prove himself right, Paul decided he would attempt to walk. He took one step, and except for the crowd's amused reactions being louder, the result was the same. Terrified, Paul dug out his cell phone and hurriedly punched in Nat's number. Even before Nat answered, Paul began to chatter incoherently.

"Paul, pull yourself together, slow down," Nat shouted into the phone.

Nat's inability to hear what Paul was screaming about was compounded by the loud laughter in the background. Something strange was going on and obviously Paul was not finding it funny.

It took much time and effort for Nat to get his hysterical friend to calm himself enough to be understood.

"Listen to me, Paul.... I know you are upset but you will be all right," Nat cajoled, speaking deliberately and enunciating clearly. "Did I hear you say that you are standing at the corner of Sixty-third and Park Avenue?"

"Yessyessssixtthirr," Paul stammered, "whachyewsed, whachyewsed!"

"Whachyewsed," Nat repeated, then translating, "What-you-said—in other words, Paul, what *I* said was correct?"

"Yessss, sssocccomessffffast assyoucn, okkkay?"

"Okay, I'll come as fast as I can. Hold tight, Paul, I'm on my way!"

Nat pocketed his cell phone and called, "Check please!"

"But Mr. Noland," the waiter noted, "you have eaten only breadsticks."

"...And they were delicious!" Nat said, dropping a twenty into the basket. "My compliments to the chef."

CHAPTER 7

As Nat exited the Bistro, a yellow cab pulled up. "Perfect!" Nat thought. "I'll leave my car and take the cab…save time looking for a parking space."

Acting the gentleman, Nat opened the cab door and watched an attractive, leggy blonde alight. She smiled at him and he smiled back.

"Sir, before you get in," she whispered sweetly, "I suggest you roll down the windows…I just left a pungent fart in there."

Nat nodded and thanked her for "the heads-up." She laughed at the term "heads-up" as he did at her rejoinder, "Don't you mean 'arses-up'?"

Nat heeded her advice, as did the driver. As they went about opening all the windows, Nat found himself chuckling over the snappy dialogue he and the blonde stranger had exchanged.

"Great scene for the book," he mumbled, "Good to drop a little toilet humor into *Blurbs*."

"Is better, she drop blurbs in toilet," the Russian-accented driver suggested. "Not smell up my taxi!"

"Blurbs, how about that!" Nat thought, taken aback. "Blurbs means 'farts' in Russian...going to have to rethink the title!"

"Uh, sir," Nat said, addressing the driver.

"Not sir...Fyodor!" the driver corrected, smiling.

"Fyodor, does 'blurbs' mean 'farts' in your language?"

"No, in *your* language...I think. Yes?"

"No, it doesn't. How do you say 'fart'?" Nat asked.

"Fart!" he answered proudly. "I pronounce good, yes?"

"You did, I meant what is the Russian word for fart?"

"Oh! Is 'vetri'. But Russian lady never say 'vetri', like the American blondie say 'fart'."

"Most American ladies don't say 'fart' either, but thank you."

Nat was happy his title was secure but worried that his friend Paul wasn't. Why had he sounded so stressed? And why would he be waiting on a street corner blathering like an idiot? Did he have a stroke? Had he been mugged, or had a drink or two with his editor? Or five?

"Mugging, heart attack, drunk, stroke, anything is possible," he thought as the taxi inched through traffic, "especially since the wild e-mailing buddy came into my life."

"It's GodGod," Nat declared, angrily, "He's the one responsible for Paul's state!"

"Excuse please, I do not know which is Paul's state," Fyodor offered, "but *president* responsible for *all* fifty state, *my* state, *Paul's* state. I blame president, not…how you say, GodGod!"

Nat had not realized he'd been talking aloud and, rather than try to explain himself, he agreed.

"You're so right. But blame our *ex*-president, good ole George W. He screwed up everything for everybody."

While Nat sat in the cab mulling over how to get GodGod out of his life, GodGod was busy sending Nat two new e-mails to ponder.

CHAPTER 8

Word travels fast in New York, especially when it's a word that promises something unusual is in the offing. By the time Nat arrived at the designated corner, the crowd's size had trebled and from their demeanor Nat gleaned that what Paul had to tell him would be bizarre, and possibly grist for his book.

He instructed Fyodor to keep his meter running while he looked about for Paul. Nat spied a bedraggled, homeless-looking man leaning against a building and shouting "Nat…Nat!?" with a hoarse version of Paul's voice. Nat ran to him and stupidly asked if he was all right.

"Do I…look like…I'm…all right?" a totally enervated Paul croaked. "I am anything but all right."

As far as Nat was concerned, Paul was a hundred percent more "all right" than the unintelligible hysteric he spoke with minutes earlier.

"Paul, does Paula know where you are and what happened to you?" Nat asked, fingering his phone. "What *did* happen to you?"

"Put that phone away!" Paul moaned, shaking his head. "*I* don't know what happened to me!"

"Shouldn't we get in touch with her?"

"No! I don't want her to see me like this. She'd be frightened and I don't want that. She's... she's pregnant, you know."

"No, I didn't," Nat said, suspicious his friend was fantasizing. "How far along is she?"

"Missed her last period.... Don't call her til I can walk!" Beckoning his friend close, Paul whispered, "Nat, do you know what happened to me?"

"No, tell me. What happened to you?"

"You!" Paul said accusingly, "You happened to me, you and your damn suggestions to God! I tasted one of your friggin' Just Desserts, that's what happened to me!"

"No, no, it can't be. That's impossible, uh... which," Nat stammered, "which suggestion?"

"The first one on your list...and why did it happen to me?"

"I don't know, Paul. Uh, what did you do?"

"Nothing!" he snapped angrily. "I didn't do one damn uncivil thing! And what the hell did you write as punishment for breaking your damn Suggestion? And what does 'walking privileges suspended' mean? And how long am I going to have to walk crazy?"

"I don't know, Paul...I—"

"How could you not know?" Paul snarled. "You invented the goddamned list!"

"Paul, all I know is what I suggested," a shocked Nat muttered. "God is the one who...what do you mean 'walked crazy'? How did you walk?"

"I didn't walk! I hopped," Paul admitted, embarrassed.

"You hopped? You mean like a bunny rabbit?" Nat shouted.

Paul's admission and Nat's explosive reaction provoked titters from the original onlookers and elicited questions from the late arrivals: "Did *you* see him hop?" "Is he going to hop again?" "Why was he hopping?"

"Why *were* you hopping?" Nat asked, suppressing a smile.

"I don't know why I was hopping, and I don't know why you're smiling!" he barked.

"Am I smiling? I guess I am. Sorry, I can explain."

Nat closed his eyes and started to sing, *"Hippity-Hop Bunny, Hippity-Hop Bunny, You're a funny bunny!"*

"If you're trying to be funny," Paul said through clenched teeth, "you're failing!"

"I'm not...I mean trying to be funny. Paul, the song "Hippity-Hop Bunny" is the song I found on my computer this morning. There was this big, pink, cartoon rabbit hopping up and down on a lawn. I think my e-mailing deity was telling me something."

"He was telling *you*, but he was *using me!* That sonofabitch God of yours had me hopping up and down like an idiot! Why the hell did he do that?"

"For laughs? Sorry, I don't know why. What can I do?"

"Tell your pal to leave me be!" Paul barked in frustration. "I can't believe I have a relationship with someone who doesn't exist but has the power to punish me, and for no damn reason!"

"You did nothing to warrant punishment?" Nat asked, as a sarcastic parent might.

"You mean, like committing an *incivility*?" Paul enunciated, mockingly.

"Incivility" and "Punishment" popped into Nat's head. He thought, "I'll bet that's what I & P stands for!"

"Did you, Paul," Nat asked coyly, "commit some sort of uncivil act?"

"Absolutely not! No! Unless He," Paul said, pointing up, "thought..."

"Unless He thought what?"

"That I grabbed a taxi that...," Paul offered reluctantly, "that somebody might have thought was theirs."

"It *was* theirs!" A burly doorman shouted. "I saw the old couple hail that cab!"

"An old couple?" Nat asked, raising an eyebrow.

"Yeah," the doorman insisted, "He darted in front of them and almost knocked them over!"

"I did not!" Paul shouted.

Eager to defend himself, Paul took a step toward the doorman, but instead of going forward he started hopping up and down in place. Nat could not believe his eyes and actually closed and opened them twice, hoping the scene would change. It did not. There was his friend Paul struggling to walk, and the more he struggled, the more rapidly and higher he hopped. Nat thought to grab him, but restrained himself, fearing that something dire might happen if he insinuated himself into the process.

"Paul," Nat shouted, "can't you stop hopping?"

"I can," he gasped, "if I stop trying to walk."

He stopped trying and came to rest a foot from where he had started.

"No matter how hard I try," Paul explained, puffing, "I can't move forward more than an inch for every hop."

"Not an efficient way to get about," Nat remarked, again failing to suppress a smile when he recalled Monty Python and the image of John Cleese illustrating his silly walk to candidates hoping to register their "silly walks" with the British Ministry of Silly Walks.

"Nat, this is not funny!" Paul scolded. "Stop grinning and do something!"

"Do what, Paul?" Nat asked soberly. "Tell me what to do!"

"For starters, you can pick me up and put me in that cab!"

"Done! Hold tight!"

Nat, snatching up his chunky friend, made the crowd giggle. With Paul cradled in his arms, Nat took a step and immediately started hopping up and down. Dwellers in neighboring buildings looked out their windows to see what had provoked the raucous laughter.

"Paul, you'll probably cover more ground… and faster," Nat explained as he put his friend down, "if you hopped on your own. Godspeed!"

Nat watched empathically as Paul high-hopped his way toward the cab. It required five long minutes to travel the fifteen feet from the building to the curb—a detail not lost on Nat, who continued to catalogue every bit of the madness for his book. "It's possible," he thought, "for *Blurbs* to develop into something even weirder than I planned."

As Nat helped his hapless friend get into the cab, the crowd laughing at Paul's plight so filled him with guilt that he shouted, "Go home, sadists, performance over!"

Save for moaning, tongue-clucking, and mournful sighing, no actual words were exchanged between Nat and Paul until the cab approached Paul's building. The first words uttered were Paul's: "Keep driving, Fyodor!"

Fyodor kept driving.

Paul's next words were mostly expletives used to rail at Nat and his conspirators for afflicting him with this "goddamned curse." He vowed never to go home and allow Paula to see him "hopping around like a friggin' pogo stick!"

"Maybe the affliction is gone," Nat said hopefully. "That thing could go as quickly as it came."

Paul considered the possibility and ordered Fyodor to "Stop the damn cab!" He got out, tried taking one step and immediately started to hop. He stopped trying, fell into the cab, and shouted, "Take Mr. Noland home!"

On the way, a bedraggled, beaten Paul suggested a possible, but unlikely, solution to his problem.

"Nat, how about this? How about," Paul said, shaking his head, "I can't believe I'm saying this, but how about if you e-mail this, this, *super being*, or whoever, and tell him, or her, that I admit to grabbing that elderly couple's cab, and I feel awful that I did, and I would like to make amends by searching them out and apologizing to them. What do you think? Will your friggin' deity cancel the curse and let me go back to my regular-style walking? And don't tell me that you have no idea."

"I *have* an idea! We go with *your* idea! An act of sincere contrition…. It should work!"

On arriving home, Nat jumped out of the cab, shouting, "GodGod has to forgive you…forgiveness is what God preaches."

"I hope it's what your guy practices!" Paul moaned.

"Fyodor," Nat said, handing him a fifty-dollar bill, "you see what's going on here. Can you hang in with us?"

"I see…and I can hang!" Fyodor agreed "I am interest what will be."

Fyodor mused, "What a country! All day, two customers...a baldy who hop and a blondie who fart!"

Paul stretched out in the back of the cab as Nat raced to get to his computer. On his way in, Nat had a quick interchange with Glennie, who was on her way out.

"Nat, why are you racing about like a madman?"

"I am trying to get GodGod to pardon Paul."

"*For what?*"

"Ask Paul...you won't believe it," he shouted, dashing down the basement stairs, "He's in the cab parked out front!"

It was not necessary for Nat to dial up GodGod because on his computer were the two messages GodGod had sent earlier. One was clear and concise, which Nat read in utter disbelief. If ever he had doubts that he was dealing with an all-knowing, all-seeing, very highest of highest powers, those doubts were forever dispelled.

In an uncharacteristically reverential tone, an awed Nat declaimed, "There are more things in Heaven and Earth, *Nat Noland*, than are dreamt of in your philosophy."

It somehow comforted Nat to speak those particular words of Shakespeare's and interpolate his name into Hamlet's musing.

Before rushing out to announce his amazing finding to the world, which at the moment consisted only of Glennie and Paul, Nat rechecked the date and time the e-mails were sent, then punched the air with his fist.

"Nattie boy, take a bow!" he said proudly. "I don't know why or how, but we have participated in the making of a modern miracle!"

CHAPTER 9

Glennie sat in the back seat of the taxi, holding Paul's hand and trying to be diplomatic.

"Paul, I am not saying that I don't believe you…. What I am saying is that it is hard for me, or I imagine anyone, to accept the idea of such a thing happening. It seems so…science fiction."

"S'cuse, Mrs. Lady, is no science fiction," Fyodor interjected, "…is *real* fiction!"

"It's no kind of fiction, Glennie," Paul insisted. "If I were able to handle another episode of involuntary hopping, I'd get in the street and prove it."

"Paul, I don't want you getting into the street and hop—"

"I do!" Nat interjected, popping his head in the window, "Paul, get out of the cab!"

"You don't have to, Paul, I believe you," Glennie said, taking his hand, "You don't have to prove anything."

"He does!" Nat insisted, opening the door. "He has to prove to himself that he can walk again!"

"Why are you saying that? Did you find out something from...?" Paul asked, warily pointing skyward.

"Yes! Listen to this," Nat said, reading from a computer printout, "'Apology accepted. Lesson learned. Seven H's Fine.' Paul, it's a miracle!"

"What is?" "What's a miracle?" Paul and Glennie asked simultaneously.

"This!" Nat said, referring to the printout.

"What does 'apology accepted, lesson learned' mean?" Paul asked.

"I would say it means that you've been forgiven and pardoned."

"And 'Seven H's Fine'…. What does that mean?"

"I'm not sure, but it has the word 'fine' in it and that bodes well," Nat insisted. "The important thing is that this is miraculous!"

"What's miraculous about it?" Paul demanded.

"What is miraculous, Paul," Nat spoke slowly, giving import to each word, "is that this message is in response to the suggestion you made to me about admitting guilt and making amends by apologizing to the old couple."

"…And so you e-mailed that to GodGod, and he e-mailed this back," Paul stated, grabbing the printout. "Where's the miracle?"

"I did not e-mail your idea to GodGod! Paul, this message was waiting for me when I got home. It was in my computer! That's the miracle! *He* read your mind!"

"He read my…?" Paul muttered, "That can't be."

"Be thankful it is! Paul, get out and walk," Nat said, holding open the cab door.

Desperately wanting to be normal again, Paul allowed Nat and Fyodor to assist him from the cab.

"I guess a glass of wine is out of the question," Paul joked, standing unsteadily between the two men. "Okay, Nat, what now?"

"Now, Paulelah, start walking!"

Paul was surprised that Nat addressed him as Paulelah, but rather than take umbrage he took heart and confidently strode forward. To the shock and chagrin of everyone but Nat, Paul started to hop.

"Oh, Nooooo!" he screamed.

"It's all right," Nat yelled, "it's all right!"

"It's not! It's not! I'm hopping!" he groaned and began to weep.

"Two, three…keep going, Paul," Nat encouraged as he counted the hops, "…four…five…you're doing great… six…just one more…seven! I think you've done it!"

And behold, on the seventh hop, Paul walked!

"I can walk, I can walk!" Paul cried out, now weeping tears of joy. "I CAN WALK!"

"*That's* what the 'Seven H's Fine' meant," Nat shouted. "You paid a *fine*...a seven-hop fine to have your walking privileges restored."

Paul walked two more steps and immediately stopped weeping and started phoning. He could now tell his wife about the horrifying adventure he had lived through. He reached Paula on her cell phone and after exchanging quick hellos, Paula asked casually, "So, how was lunch, dear? Anything interesting happen?"

"Oh, I don't know that you would call it interesting," Paul offered, grinning mischievously, "but Nat and I spent a pretty goofy afternoon...if you have a minute?"

"I don't, darling. Clyde is about to blow me."

"Blow-*dry*!" Paula's hairdresser shrieked into the phone. "Mr. Bluett, your wife is sooo naughty!"

"I'll try to behave!" Paula laughed. "See you later, dear."

Paul, struggling with mixed emotions, screamed, "You can blow-dry my ass, bitch!"

Then to Nat's surprise, Paul smiled and blew a kiss into the phone.

"Paul, are you okay?" Nat asked cautiously.

"Rest easy, Nat, I *am* okay…a damn lot 'okayer' than I've been for a long time. I admit that when Paula said she didn't have time to hear about our goofy day, I felt like screaming 'Blow-dry my ass, you bitch,' but luckily I restrained myself."

Nat thought, "Oh, boy, the man's in trouble. All that high-hopping has rattled his brain."

"Paul," Nat advised calmly, "you actually did not restrain yourself. You did tell Paula that she was a bitch and to blow-dry your ass."

"I would never, ever say such a thing to her," a hurt Paul insisted.

"Paul, you said it to her…not two minutes ago."

"I did *not* say it to her…I…"

"You did, Paul! Fyodor, did you hear?"

"I hear, yes!" Fyodor concurred. "Is no business of me, but I hear Mister say, 'Blow my dry ass, bitch!'"

"Will you both shut up and listen!" Paul snapped. "I did not say it to *her*…. I said it to her cell-phone…*after* she had hung up on me. Her hanging up on me made me furious, but only for a second. Did you also hear me blow a kiss into her dead phone?"

"Yes."

"Bingo! Thinking of how pretty her hair is made me horny. Anything else, Nat?"

"Yeah, how did you go from furious to horny so fast?"

"Tell Fyodor to take me home, and I'll explain."

"I take you!" Fyodor said, starting his motor.

"Okay, Paul," Nat said as the cab pulled away from the curb, "explain!"

"My fury left seconds after I realized that I did not want to tell her about our goofy afternoon. I don't want to tell anybody about this nightmarish day nor do I intend to write about it in my column, and I would hope that our goofy afternoon doesn't turn up in your new...what are you calling it?"

"*Blurbs*...and it won't, if you feel that strongly about it...but—"

"But?" Paul asked, pouncing on the word. "Why did you say 'but'?"

"Did I say 'but'?" Nat asked naively. "I didn't mean to."

"Nobody ever says 'but' who doesn't mean to," Paul argued.

"Well, I didn't mean to say 'but'...I...I meant to say, 'however.'"

"You meant to say 'but' and got caught in a lie! Admit it!" Paul pushed.

"Okay, I admit it...but I could have said 'however.' The truth is I didn't mean to say either out loud. I thought I was thinking 'but.' I talk to myself, you know that...cut me a little slack, frchrissakes.... Look at that, this is the second time today I said 'frchrissakes', and I never..."

Suddenly Nat felt spent. He had been caught lying, and his only option now was contrition.

"I'm sorry, Paul, I guess I could have said 'however' to make my point."

"What is your point?"

"*Our*, is my point. Your reference to *our* goofy afternoon. Granted, it did start as *your* goofy afternoon, but when I became involved, it changed, and I think it is patently unfair to ask me to give up my literary rights to *Our* Goofy Afternoon."

Fyodor announcing. "Okay, we here!" stopped Paul from further debating the issue. After insisting Fyodor accept an extra ten-dollar tip, Paul got out of the cab.

"Thank you," Fyodor declared, "You both fine gentlemens."

The "fine gentlemens" exchanged cursory goodnights, Paul adding, "We'll talk later."

To keep from jeopardizing their relationship, Nat had decided not to further engage Paul on the subject. He had already earmarked a full chapter to Paul's hopping affliction, and since he was, in great measure, responsible for Paul being punished and for his return to normalcy, Nat could not in fairness to his art exclude this mind-blowing material from his novellelah.

"I owe it to humanity," Nat told himself, "and to God knows who else."

CHAPTER 10

Nat came home to an eerily quiet house and Glennie's ultra-cheery voice on the answering machine informing him that she and the girls would be sleeping at their cousins' so their parents could have a romantic night out.

"I hope I'm not inconveniencing you, dear," she cooed.

"Inconveniencing me?" he yipped. "Darling, you are *conveniencing* me…and I thank you!"

Nat needed time alone to sort out what in his weird life needed priority attention. He had been girding himself to deal with the disquieting e-mail GodGod had been sending him.

To further complicate his life, Nat found, sitting atop his computer, a letter from someone he feared and expected would contact him one day.

"But why now?" Nat muttered, "And how the hell did he get my address?"

"Dear Mr. Noland," the letter read, "I have learned from our mutual friend R.K. that you have used my name to promote your new novel. Your

writing glowing quotes for a book that does not yet
exist and attributing them to known authors is, I'll
grant, an original idea, and an appalling one. It is also
illegal and actionable. Be warned, sir, that I will sue
should you persist in putting your words into my
mouth. Larry Gelbart."

Nat dropped his head into his hands. "How
could this happen," he thought, "and why is it
happening to me? And who is this mutual friend R.K.
who fed Larry Gelbart those pages? Who, with the
initials R.K., hates me?"

"Robert Kennedy," he shouted suddenly.
"He's the only R.K. I know...and I never met him,
and he's dead...so why would he hate me?!"

Nat heard himself talking nonsense and it
frightened him. He was slowly losing his grip on
reality—his once-sharp mental processes were
slowly eroding and his thinking was becoming
increasingly muddled. His ability to use basic logic
had all but disappeared. He began to realize how
serious things were when he failed to do something
he had done every day of his life—talk things over
with himself. So Nat tried asking himself a simple
question out loud:

"Hey, Nat, shouldn't we find out who R.K. is
before we include Gelbart's letter in the book?"

When there was no response after three attempts, he tried a new approach.

"Nat," he said, speaking very softly, "you are thinking and listening, aren't you? I know you are because I have done the same thing. So, Nat, just stop thinking and listening...and start talking. We're a team and team members *have* to talk! I'll make it easy...just follow my lead."

"Hello, Nat, how are you?" he said, as if to a child.

After repeating several simple variations of the question and getting no response, he felt a deep sense of abandonment and, in desperation, peppered himself with all manner of pleas, requests and outright orders:

"Nat, talk to me!" he implored, "Nat, Nat, where are you? Say something, Nat, please! Nat, why don't you answer me? What's gotten into you, Nat? Whatever the hell it is, snap out of it! Talk, Nat, talk!... Damn it, Nat, tell me to go screw myself!... Screw you, Nat!"

All of Nat's exhortations, cajoling, and demands went unanswered.

"Nat," he addressed himself sadly, "do you realize that you have lost a member of your writing team, your best collaborator? And so have I! Face it, Nat!"

"Face it, Nat! Face it, *Nat?*" he repeated, emphasizing his name.

Nat suddenly started to grin. He had, inadvertently, pinpointed his problem and in doing so had found its solution.

"I am such a dope!" he said, slapping his forehead, "*Nat*, I have been saying, '*Nat*, talk to me!' 'Hello, *Nat*' and 'How are you, *Nat?*' I, like an idiot, have been trying to talk to *me*, Nat! *I* am Nat! How stupid! It took me a while, but I got it...okay, let's start all over."

"Hello, *Nattie!*" he offered happily, "*Nattie*, I've been calling you Nat, and you are obviously 'Nattie' or 'Nattie boy.' You know I never thought it mattered which one of us was which...the important thing is that we talked things over...and boy, do we have a lot to talk over. This whole GodGod e-mail has me crazy, Nattie. You too?"

The longer Nat spoke, the more depressed he became. He was not ready to accept the fact that, for whatever reason, Nat and Nattie were no longer on speaking terms.

What frightened Nat as much as losing his ability to converse with himself was losing his grip on reality, and what further terrified him was not knowing exactly which reality he was losing his grip on! Was it the reality he shared with Glennie and the twins, or the literary reality he shared with his computer and publisher—or was it the newfound spiritual reality he shared with GodGod and his ministering angel R.K.?

How did he get into this mess...or *who* had gotten him into it? He thought of the genesis of *Blurbs*—and how he had started it as a follow-up to his last novel. Besides himself, Paul Bluett, and GodGod (a.k.a. R.K, the unknown source who ratted him out to Larry Gelbart), who else had access to *Blurbs*? Now that he had no confidant, no one with whom he could converse, no one whose advice he could trust, who then might he turn to?

"Ross Davidoff!" he thought. "I could talk things over with him."

Ross Davidoff was his editor at Stern and Hanft and, in fact, the most solid, stolid, no-nonsense, straight-talking, honest person he knew. "Why not?" he thought. "I haven't told him about my new book.... I can tell him about *Blurbs*."

Somehow making a simple decision to contact a pragmatic, supportive, civilized businessman had a therapeutic effect on Nat. He calmly picked up the phone, speed-dialed a number, and waited to hear Ross Davidoff's secretary, McKensie, say, "Ross

Davidoff's office. Can you hold?" McKensie did not disappoint. Nat held for five seconds and in ten was talking to an upbeat Ross Davidoff.

"Nat, I'm so happy to hear your voice," he sang. "I hope you're calling to tell me about a new novel."

"Well, that's one of the reasons. How did you know I started a new novel? Well, it's not exactly new, and it's not a novel...exactly."

"Oh? So what is your 'not exactly new...not a novel exactly' about?"

"Actually, Ross, this book was inspired by something I started years ago...*God Help Me Help You.*"

"Oh, yes, you sent me some pages.... "

"I did, Ross, and you weren't impressed."

"If I recall," Ross Davidoff said, grimacing, "I said it stunk."

"'...To high heavens was your full comment. But, Ross," Nat said defensively, "it's quite different now. Our hero doesn't write God letters.... He e-mails God, and the surprise is that God e-mails him back. I know it sounds weird, but I was going for weird. I wanted to satirize those left-behind rapture books...in mine nobody gets left behind. They all stay and find heaven on earth. I'm hoping that my..."

"Nat," Ross interrupted, "what you're telling me is…?"

"…is that I am writing a strange, convoluted story with many diverse elements," Nat said, selling hard."Elements which include aspects of theism, atheism and a lot of 'meism.' At its core is a man's intensely personal search for truth and sanity through spirituality. Ross, the book is definitely unconventional. It has like two motors driving it… you could call it a…*hybrid*."

"I see…. Nat," the publisher spoke hesitantly, "tell me a little about your…hybrid."

Nat was able, in a few sentences, to describe how he had jump-started *Blurbs* by writing his own quotes praising his unwritten novel and attributing them to unwitting celebrities.

Ross Davidoff seemed taken aback, and to make certain he heard right, he repeated what Nat had told him and then asked Nat to describe the book's premise, its major characters, their problems, and the story's development.

Nat was *excited* to find such a willing ear and spoke energetically and at length about what he had on paper and was planning to add, and how he had no idea how it would end or what the denouement might be, adding, "But one thing I can guarantee…it'll get people talking!"

Ross listened intently, never once interrupting to ask a question or seek clarification. Nat ended his presentation by reading to him the book's preface and the Larry Gelbart suit-threatening letter he had received that day.

"Ross, I'm going to include Mr. Gelbart's letter in the book," Nat boasted. "There's nothing like a lawsuit to pique the public's interest."

Nat waited anxiously for his publisher's response. Given Ross Davidoff's negative assessment of the source material, Nat expected to hear, "It still stinks!"

Whatever Ross Davidoff's thoughts were—negative or positive—they were not forthcoming. What Nat heard was stony silence, and after too many seconds of soundlessness, a discomforted Nat dared to ask, "So, Ross, what do you think?"

"Nat, I...I...," Ross Davidoff answered hesitantly, "...I will get back to you."

Ross Davidoff's unresponsiveness and his hanging up while Nat was starting to ask, "How soon do you think that'll be?" did nothing for Nat's fragile ego, nor did Ross Davidoff's not calling back immediately to explain himself.

Nat sat at his desk and stared despairingly at the phone. In all the years they had known each other, Nat never imagined that Ross Davidoff, his good and supportive friend, would suddenly turn negative on him. He considered calling him and yelling, "What the hell flew up your ass, Buddy?" but instead he yelled it at a strange, menacing man he saw staring at him in his shaving mirror. For a split second, Nat was unaware he was yelling at himself— he looked that bad...that different. He had scared himself, and to keep from scaring others he reached for his three-headed Norelco and began to shave. He hoped that getting rid of the two-day growth would render him less fearsome and unattractive and might even afford a degree of protection from himself and from *them*. "Them" being the men he was sure would soon be coming to take him to a mental institution.

"They're apt to be gentler handling me," he reasoned, "if I don't look as confused and crazy as I feel."

He checked his clean-shaven image in the mirror and saw someone he had never seen before.

"Integrated," he thought. "I am looking at an integrated man."

He continued to look into the mirror and, for the first time ever, did not give voice to the ritual exchange he had with himself after his morning shave. Left unsaid were:

"You look great, Nattie!"

"And so do you, Nat."

CHAPTER 11

T hroughout his illustrious career Ross Davidoff had hundreds of phone conversations with every stripe of author, from the old wizened ones to the eager first-timers. Most calls were routine, some were heated, but all were civil. Never in his twenty-two years as an executive at Stern and Hanft had he ever, for any reason, hung up on any of his authors or, for that matter, on anybody—until today. Today he had no choice but to hang up because what he had heard rendered him speechless. That Nat Noland, whose five novels he had been proud to publish and whom he considered a personal friend, would blatantly plagiarize someone else's work and try to pass it off as his own was unthinkable and totally unexpected.

Ross Davidoff could not believe his ears when he heard Nat read the book's preface and then tell how his central character e-mailed suggestions to God on how to improve the world...and God e-mailed back. Nat had not only plagiarized a work Ross knew intimately, but he had made sorry attempts to disguise the act by changing a word or two in the preface. It was blatant plagiarism. For a brief moment the editor considered that *Just Desserts* might have been plagiarized from *Blurbs,* but when Nat admitted that he had written about forty pages, but did not quite know how it would end, Ross Davidoff knew what the truth was. *Just Desserts* was not any further along, but the author had a good idea how it would end and said that it was one of the most satisfying of any of his works to date.

Ross Davidoff had neither the heart nor the disposition to confront Nat with the disturbing evidence that *Blurbs* was a blatant rip-off of the manuscript he was now holding in his hands. Though Ross Davidoff had told Nat that he would "get back" to him, he knew he could not. It would be too painful to phone Nat and inform him that, because he had crossed the line, Stern and Hanft would no longer publish this or any of his future works. Much less painful, he decided, would be to e-mail this message to Nat. The irony of using an e-mail was not lost on Ross Davidoff, who was set to make a deal to publish *Just Desserts*, a novel where e-mailing was so integral to the story.

Ross hoped that Nat had some credible, exculpatory explanation for his actions, but he sincerely doubted it.

He fired up his computer, typed in Nat's e-mail address, natnol@aol.com, and before writing the note, he hesitated to consider what the manner and tone of his message should be. He concluded that rather than accusing Nat of being a plagiarist, he would get Nat to admit that he was one.

CHAPTER 12

A full day had passed, and Nat was pissed. No longer needing to discuss things with himself out loud, Nat made the unilateral decision to phone Ross and demand to know why he had hung up on him. He was a heartbeat away from picking up the phone and asking, "Why the hell did you hang up on me, shithead, and when were you planning to get back to me…St. Crispin's day?" He was considering his options when Glennie came breezing into the bedroom carrying a bundle of assorted mail.

Knowing what a sleepless night Nat had had and how vulnerable he was, she dreaded being the bearer of bad tidings, which her intuition told her she was about to be.

"Darling," she offered casually, "There's an overnight in there from Stern and Hanft.

"It's that large manila one," she added, dashing out while Nat was picking up the envelope.

Glennie preferred to get a debriefing *after* Nat had read and reacted to whatever it was his publisher had sent. If he were provoked to blow off steam, she found he fared better when he was allowed to do his initial venting in private.

Nat hefted the package and wondered what Davidoff had sent him. "It's not like Ross to spring surprises on me," he thought. "Neither was it to hang up on me."

"Nothing," he concluded, "is like it once was."

"That's for damn sure," he mumbled as he tore open the package that contained a manuscript and a printout of an e-mail from Ross Davidoff addressed to: natnol@aol.com.

"Something askew is going on here," he thought as he read aloud:

"Dear Nat, Enclosed are forty pages of a manuscript our company has been developing. I expect the final draft to be delivered in a few weeks. You should be able to read it in an hour…it's going to be a noveletta."

Nat stopped reading and sucked in three short gulps of air before continuing.

"I was quite smitten with the writing," Nat read quickly, his lip curling as he raced on. "However, I have reservations about the premise and am a bit leery of its commercial value. It's entitled *Just Desserts* and was written by Rhyne Karlner. Let me know what you think. Sincerely, Ross."

"What I think?" Nat exploded. "You want to know what I think, Mr. Davidoff? I think you are a lying, thieving, shithead scavenger!" Nat screamed, slapping at the e-mail printout, "You and your thieving, bastard buddy, this Rhyne Karlner, are ripping me off!

Nat ranted on, "*A noveletta?* Rhyne the Ripper ripped it off from 'novellelah'...a word I invented, and *Just Desserts* he ripped off from the alternate title I was considering for *Blurbs*! You two thieving sonsofabitches!

"Glennie!" Nat shouted up the stairway, "I'm being ripped off! I'm being plagiarized! Glennieeee, where are youuuuu?"

Glennie was in her car and starting out. She heard Nat calling but decided not to answer. She knew her husband. He would only get angrier if someone were with him telling him to calm down. Hopefully, during the stormy half hour she would be gone, he will have talked it over with himself. She was envious of his ability to defuse his inner bombs by chatting with his alter ego, which she did not realize was no longer an option for him. Nat chose not to tell her about this development, in fear that she would think his mental unraveling was further along than it appeared to be.

Nat angrily punched in Glennie's cell phone number then quickly slammed it down.

"I could never forgive myself," he thought, "if my stupid, out-of-control ranting caused her to have an accident on her way to pick up our kids."

Nat felt good that he could still be concerned about the things that really mattered in life and immediately went back to dealing with what really, really mattered—the two bastards who had stolen his mind. With his thumb and forefinger he gingerly picked up the *Just Desserts* manuscript and, with his nose poised to expect a foul odor, opened to the preface and quickly scanned it. He was appalled to find that, with very minor differences, it was identical to the one he had written for *Blurbs*.

Preface

For more than two-hundred centuries, a great portion of the world's population has accepted the belief that if you lived an ethical and moral life here on earth, your soul would be welcomed by God into the Kingdom of Heaven and there live on in eternal peace. But if you chose to live an amoral life, the Devil would arrange that you burn for eternity in a fiery Hell. At twelve I started to wonder about the concept of a fiery hell. Against my mother's advice, I confronted our minister. "If I could burn for eternity," I dared suggest to Reverend Goodleigh, "wouldn't that make me like, immortal? And isn't being immortal a good thing to be?"

Reverend Goodleigh smiled benignly and asked, "Rhyne, have you ever been burned?" When I told him that my father's cigarette ash once fell on my arm, and the pain was real, real, bad, he asked sweetly, "Well, Rhyne, can you imagine that real, real bad pain multiplied a trillion-trillion times and suffering with that real, real bad pain for eternity?" When I told him that I couldn't imagine it, he smiled, tapped his Bible and said, "Of course you can't, Rhyne! But it is something to think about, isn't it, son?"

"That no talent, plagiarizing punk!" Nat railed, throwing the manuscript to the floor. "You see what that shithead did, God? That rip-off artist changed my first line, 'For more than two thousand years' to 'for more than two-hundred centuries.' I used the phrase, 'against the exhortations of my mother,' and he changes it to, 'against my mother's advice.' Hah? That Rhyne rip-off artist changes my actual minister's name, 'Reverend Raleigh' to 'Reverend Goodleigh.' Big friggin' improvement!

"And look at this, God," Nat said, showing the page to the ceiling. "I wrote a 'million-billion' times, and he changed it to 'a trillion-trillion' and his niggling change here to 'cigarette' ash from the original 'cigar' ash, which is what my father smoked. What pisses me off more than anything is that he changes 'Nat,' my name, the guy who actually had that conversation with Minister Raleigh, to Rhyne, his plagiarizing name. Well, he's not going to get away with stealing my identity and neither are you, Mr. Ross Davidoff!"

Nat snatched up the manuscript he had thrown to the floor and shouted at it, "How many more indignities are in this lie you plan to publish, Ross?"

Nat cracked the book open and started to read.

> *Through the years he continued to wonder why so many millions of good and loving people have bought the theory of "Eternal Peace in Heaven" and "Eternal Torment in a Fiery Hell" just because some silver-haired, Bible-brandishing cleric*

swore it was so. He wondered, too, if
there were a God, what would He
think of all this?

"Oh, damn them!" Nat winced and repeated the lines, "He wondered, too, if there were a God," then shouted, "Those are my words from chapter two. My words! Those unprincipled bastards!" He stopped in mid-curse when his eye caught the next two words in the paragraph—it was his name. What were they up to? He read on, mesmerized.

Nat Noland questioned the
universal acceptance of Heaven and
Hell. "Why should I assume," he
asked himself, "that when my time
came, I and the scores who had
chosen the righteous way would enter
the Kingdom of Heaven? There is no
way of knowing whether or not I
would...is there?"

Nat pinched his cheek hard to assure himself that he was awake. He thought, "Those are words I wrote for *God Help Me Help You,* and they're attributing them to Nat Noland, the author, not Jim Boland, the character in the novel. What the hell are they trying to do?"

Nat continued, nodding in agreement with everything he had once written and was now reading aloud.

> *What irritated Mr. Noland even more was not knowing the fate of all the amoral, conscienceless perpetrators of cruelty. Would they, in fact, be spending eternity in the fiery hell they were promised? Nat Noland thought, "It would be nice to know that all evil-doers got their just desserts."*
>
> *Yesterday morning, as Nat sat on a bench in Franklin Park hoping to add to his list of Suggestions to God, he heard angry shouting. He turned to see a large, angry man dragging a cowering five-year-old-boy by the arm and warning him to "stop blubbering like a spoiled brat or he would get a whacking he wouldn't forget." And he was right—neither the boy nor Nat would ever forget that brutal assault. Seeing the stream of blood that gushed from the child's nose and mouth sent Nat into a rage. He recalled the clarity of the language he had just added to*

Suggestion #2 from his list of Just Desserts and found it applicable!

"Should any adult act inhumanely to any child, a cluster of festering boils will break out on the adult's body and there remain until his family, his friends, employers, and all members of his community have seen his affliction and shunned him, for they will know why he is deserving of this punishment!"

When the brute answered his bloodied son's sobbing plea, "Daddy, no more, no more!" with a backhand wallop to his face, Nat jumped to his feet, raised his arms skyward and, at the top of his lungs, implored God to act! "God, implement Suggestion #2!"

And lo and behold, He acted! And the punishment began! It was awesome and disgusting...beyond anything Nat had ever witnessed in his lifetime. From the heavens, as Nat expected, a blinding shaft of the whitest, white light encircled the father! His clenched fist was frozen an inch from his son's face which, miraculously, was no longer bloody. What Nat saw happening to the father made him shudder. Pus-laden, festering boils slowly broke out on the father's fist, then on his wrist, then on both hands and wrists and arms. Terrified and trembling, the father stared at his grotesquely swollen hands and started to whimper. When he touched the pus-oozing boils that were forming on his face, a blood-curdling scream escaped from him and reverberated throughout the park. It nearly deafened Nat. It was a sound so piercing and so heart-rending that it sent birds flying out of trees and squirrels scurrying across fields.

Nat dropped the manuscript, dropped to his knees, and desperately tried not to faint.

He failed.

CHAPTER 13

Nat was more than a little surprised to find himself seated at his desk and staring at his computer screen.

"What am I doing here...?" he thought, "...and how did I get here? The last thing I remember was sitting in a park and watching birds and squirrels behaving as if the world were coming to an end. What the heck caused them to go berserk? They must have seen or heard something pretty awful to have scared them like that. I must have seen or heard it too because I think I fainted. What the heck could it have been? Did I really faint, or did I dream I fainted? That's it! Why would I be sitting in the park? I've got a book to finish. I don't have time to sit in a park. It was a dream, and I fainted in it because it was a nightmare dream...that's it!" "Or was it?" was his hesitant afterthought.

"Glennie," he called over the intercom, "last night, did I have a particularly restless night?"

"Oh, yes, you were very active."

"How active?"

"Nat, you don't remember what happened last night?" Glennie asked cautiously.

"I remember you saying, 'Nat, wake up. You're dreaming.' You did say that last night, didn't you?"

"Last night and the night before. Uh, why?"

"Just checking. Thanks, dear!"

Satisfied that his sanity was still intact, Nat got back to business, and this morning his business was to inform the parasitic cabal of plagiarist puppeteers that he was cutting their manipulating strings.

He had to get back in control and was poised to tap in: GodGod@godhelpmehelpyou.now, when the computer dinged to alert him of an incoming message.

Before looking, he knew it was from GodGod. Somehow GodGod always beat him to the punch, but today he was primed to counter punch and drop GodGod in his tracks. On the screen, Nat read:

> *Nat, we have news that will be of exceptional interest to you. I know you think we're parasites and plagiarists, and you would like to punch us out.*

Nat turned from the screen and shut his eyes. GodGod was still a step ahead of him. He opened them quickly to learn how overmatched he was:

Good, Nat…keep your eyes open. I know you think that we're working at cross-purposes, but we are not. After you fainted in the park, it was R. K. who gathered you up and took you home. And the dream you think you had last night about the boy whose cruel father's body became infested with pus-laden boils? Well, it actually occurred yesterday afternoon, and you did witness it, and you did faint!

This time Nat did not turn from the screen—he kissed it. What he never dreamt would happen, happened, and he was alive to witness it.

"I am still here," he thought, "and if this is reality, which I have every reason to believe it is, then God has successfully implemented two of the three suggestions I made to him. I wonder if people will know of this."

Nat turned to the screen and, with mounting excitement, he read:

Yes, Nat, God has successfully implemented two of the three suggestions you made to him, and the world will know of it.

"I was thinking just that!" Nat sighed and asked resignedly, "How can you hear someone thinking?"

It's a gift. But more important, answer me this, Nat. Are you still spiritually committed to the building of a brave new world, and are you ready for some good news?

"Why ask me questions you know my answers to?" Nat shouted in frustration. "You know I am desperately ready for any good news! What is it?"

It's very good news! Your third suggestion to God, the one dealing with punishment for those who tell lies which affect the well being of others…?

"Yes, yes!" Nat answered, his pulse quickening.

Well, Nat Noland, God will implement that third suggestion as soon as an offender or offenders are discovered and deemed deserving of the punishment you have outlined. Then, almost immediately, the Heaven on Earth you envisioned will become a reality, and your dream will be fulfilled. You, Nat, will have been the catalyst for the creation of a brave new world, and your life will be validated.

Nat was thunderstruck.

"How did this happen?" he asked himself. "How did I, by attempting to write a semi-serious novel, become the catalyst for the creation of a better world and thus fulfill a dream I don't remember dreaming, and also validate a life that I never thought needed validation?"

CHAPTER 14

After accepting the awesome responsibility of visiting the wrath of God upon deserving offenders, Nat felt that his life as he knew it would never be the same. The list of things he no longer had the time to do continued to grow. He no longer had time to lie with the twins at bedtime and read stories or invent tales of gentle horror for them, nor did he have the time or energy to lie with Glennie and satisfy either of their needs. He had no time to eat…and had no memory of eating anything since the nine breadsticks he gobbled down at the Bistro waiting for Paul Bluett to show. It seemed that their aborted lunch and Paul's hopping about the street happened eons ago.

Tonight, after kissing Glennie goodnight and getting into a comfortable snuggle position, Nat felt a pull to check his computer for e-mails. He resisted until Glennie dozed off…then, without waking her, disentangled himself from her arms and legs.

On his computer screen three e-mails awaited his attention. He deleted the two ads offering bargain-priced Viagra pills and opened the third, which was for *The New York Times*. It featured a photo of past and present world leaders who were scheduled to meet that following day to begin a three-day symposium on the state of the world. Nat was about to delete it when his eye was drawn to the caption and its tiny-lettered, tailing message: THE WORLD WILL BE WATCHING THESE MEN AND SO WILL NAT NOLAND.

Nat knew immediately why his name was electronically inserted into the news item. GodGod and Rhyne Karlner were calling him to arms.

An eerie calm settled over Nat. He knew *what* he had to do, with *who(m)* he would do it, *why* he was doing it and *when*. To find out the *where*, he checked the news article and learned that the symposium would be in the Assembly Hall of the United Nations, and former president George W. would represent the United States on the panel.

"I have established the 'who, what, why, when and where!'" he thought. "If I pull it off, it will be a journalistic triumph for me and a blockbuster news item for all the morning papers!"

To wish him Godspeed, the gods of passion paid a special visit to the Nolands that night. When Nat returned to his bed, Glennie had just awakened from an erotic dream and was up and wanting. After one serious kiss from her warm lips, Nat too was up and giving. For a full fifteen minutes they were extraordinarily good company for each other, and for the following six hours Nat slept more soundly than he had since he was nine weeks old.

CHAPTER 15

A clear-headed Nat thought of the monumental task on today's to-do list and was confident that he had satisfactorily covered "the who, what, why, when and where" of it but did not have the slightest idea of "how." *How* he would facilitate the implementation of his third suggestion to God was of major concern. He was more than willing to play his part, but he desperately needed guidance, and so, for the first time in his life, he actually prayed to God—his personal one.

"GodGod," he shouted, descending the stairs to his office, "this is me, and this is the first and last time I will pray to anyone unless you e-mail me a detailed set of instructions of how to proceed. If you don't, I will go back to being an atheist...a *militant* atheist."

When he saw his computer light blinking away, Nat surmised that he had gotten through. He clicked on his e-mail and there it was...his prayer, word for word with a double exclamation point after "*militant atheist!!*" He was not aware he had delivered his threat so forcefully and thought, "GodGod and R.K. obviously know me better than I know myself."

"GodGod and R.K., if you're listening," Nat said, addressing the screen, "how the heck am I supposed to get into the United Nations' Assembly? And what do I do when I get there?"

Nat looked at the screen for an answer and it came—not only in print, but also by voice...a familiar-sounding voice.

"How you get in is simple," the voice informed him. "A press pass bearing your name will be issued and delivered to your mailbox. It will give you access to the section reserved for journalists. When the floor is opened for questions, raise your hand and ask *the* question...the one that will cull the liars from the pack."

"Hold on...," Nat argued. "Why would these world leaders pick me to ask *any* question?"

"Have faith that they will," the familiar voice said, "and they will."

"And if they don't?" Nat asked.

"Then find another way!"

"But if I can't find *any* way?"

"You will!"

"How do you know?"

"Because it is important to *you* that you do."

"Important to *me*?" a frustrated Nat screamed at the screen. "How do *you* know what's important to *me*?"

"I know," the voice answered simply, "because I am you!"

With that the computer screen went blank—as did Nat's brain. He stared at the computer, then turned and looked into his shaving mirror, not sure who would be looking back at him.

"Well, Nat," he sighed, addressing himself in the mirror, "GodGod thinks he's you. I don't know who *you* are, I don't know who *I* am, and I don't know who *he* is. Apparently I don't know my ass from my elbow! Or which end is up. *Or shit from Shinola...and ten thousand other things!*"

With that Nat let out his comic, maniacal laugh, turned from the mirror, and started to type:

*A FEW OF THE 10,000 THINGS
I DON'T KNOW*

I don't know:

1. What's good on T.V. tonight.
2. Which water glass is mine.
3. Why people can't be nice.
4. What I should have for breakfast.

> 5. *What the square root of nine is.*
> 6. *Who gives a good goddamn.*
> 7. *Whose deal is it?*
> 8. *Who ate my pickle?*
> 9. *Why there's never a cop when you need one.*
> 10. *Who farted?*
> 11. *Who got us into this war?*
> 12. *Which tie I should wear.*
> 13. *Who gives a shit?*

Nat stopped when he heard a familiar voice say, "Nat Noland…. He gives a shit!"

He looked into the mirror and saw himself nodding. The familiar voice was right! He did give a shit, and if he did nothing he would agonize about it. He didn't quite know how to do what he knew he must, but, damn it, he was going to do it!

Before starting on his appointed rounds, Nat knew that if he were to represent the good in human beings, it was important to present the best possible version of himself. With that, he showered longer than usual, shampooing twice and using his wife's conditioner to add "dazzling sparkle" to his hair. He lathered his stubble of a beard in the hot shower and used the highly publicized, new, six-bladed, swivel-headed, nick-proof, Astral razor that promised the smoothest, closest shave in the history of faces. That promise, he learned after checking his face in the magnifying mirror on the vanity table, was a promise fulfilled. He hoped his prospects for success today were as glowing as his cheeks.

Nat trotted to the kitchen where he treated himself to a bowl of Honey Cheerios in skim milk, a cup of nonfat blueberry yogurt, and a mug of Postum.

Before dressing for the occasion, he checked his mailbox for the press pass. He was not going to shine his black oxford shoes, or put on his elegant gray suit and regimental tie if there were no press pass. He half hoped that GodGod and R.K. had goofed…but not only had they delivered a press pass, they had secured one from *The New York Times*—a laminated pass that sported his name and his photo!

Nat, armed with the knowledge that he had such good and powerful allies, strengthened his resolve to ferret out the influential liars of the world and have them suffer their "Just Desserts."

CHAPTER 16

The Statue of Liberty and the United Nations were the last of two New York landmarks that Nat had always planned to visit, and this morning, due to the oddest of circumstances, he would get to cross the United Nations off his "to-visit" list. If Nat were successful in his endeavor, the United Nations' building, which once promised to be the most important building in the world, would today fulfill that promise.

As he walked into the marble lobby with *The New York Times* press pass pinned to his lapel, he thought of the old black-and-white movies where the hero faked being a reporter by writing "PRESS" on a piece of cardboard and sticking it in the hatband of his fedora. He worried that the uniformed guards checking passes might toss him out as they had done to the hero in that old movie, but before he had time to create an alternative plan, a guard waved him in.

"Mr. Noland," the guard offered, "two of your colleagues from the *Times* just checked in."

"Oh, did they?" was all Nat could think to say.

"Dowd and Krugman," a woman reporter, in line behind him, interjected. "I was surprised to see them here."

'Well, I'm not," Nat said, vamping. "Uh, our editor heard that a big story might be popping, and he wanted to have his top journalists present... and me," he smiled modestly, "a humble social psychologist."

Nat moved forward quickly to abort any questions about "social psychology."

"Maureen Dowd *and* Paul Krugman," Nat thought, "*The Times's* ace editorialists! GodGod must have gotten word to their editor that this event was worthy of special attention. I'd better not louse up."

Before choosing a seat in the press box set up to accommodate hundreds of reporters, Nat looked about for the bona fide *New York Times* reps, so he might place himself as far from them as possible. He had no trouble spotting the attractive, red-headed Maureen Dowd, and, as he watched, she and a gentleman he assumed was Paul Krugman settled into first row seats. Nat sat himself down in the last row.

Nat was impressed at how quickly, at the sound of a gavel, the mass of milling, murmuring people were able to find their places and come to order. As quiet settled in the chamber filled to capacity with former and present heads of state, international dignitaries, and the general public, Nat was able to relax enough to appreciate the majesty of his surroundings. He recalled the array of colorful flags displayed at the entrance to the building and how similarly they reacted to the strong winds blowing in on them from the East River.

"Would it not be a perfect world," Nat thought, "if the member nations who were represented by those windblown flags could react with such unanimity and grace when dealing with each other in matters economic, political, and religious?"

Nat jotted down, "wind blow flags." He did not know where in *Blurbs* he might use this, but he thought it worth noting.

The event chairman, Pannit Nahari, stood at the podium between two giant screens on which his kindly face was being seen by the hundreds assembled in the hall as well as the millions throughout the world watching on television. A banner hung on the wall directly behind him which read: "1st Annual Symposium on the State of the World."

The Chairman, speaking slowly with a lilting Indian cadence, welcomed everyone to what he described as, "a singular and most important occasion."

"It is entirely possible," he continued, pausing to look directly at individual members of the assembly, "that all who are privileged to be in this chamber may be a party to an exchange of ideas and suggestions that can change the course of history!"

As Pannit Nahari spoke, Nat's awareness of his responsibility was underscored by the Chairman's looking up toward the press section and seemingly addressing the final words of his statement directly to him. The words, "will change the course of history," reverberated in his head and brought him a sense of calm—a calm which surprised and confused him.

"How can it be," he wondered, "that I am both calm and confused?"

He concluded that he was *confused* only as to when or how he would make happen what GodGod insisted needed to happen and *calm* because he believed he would find a way...with or without GodGod's help.

As the chairman droned on about the day's procedure, Nat checked the press handout that he had found on his seat. It was the day's agenda...and there was but one subject:

WARS

1. Past Wars: What led to them
2. Current Wars: How to end them
   immediately and fairly
3. Future Wars: How to avoid them

The Chairman called upon each of the leaders to bring the assembly up-to-date on any conflicts in which their countries were now involved—and what solution, if any, might end these hostilities. Nat listened attentively to all the distinguished speakers. He wanted to believe that our former President, the former Russian President, the current Prime Ministers of France and Great Britain, and the other distinguished heads of state could be taken at their word—that they were all opposed to war and would never consider it as the first option for their country to settle a dispute.

All made eloquent and convincing arguments for their reluctant, but necessary, involvement in current or past conflicts. However, midway through one of the speeches, something happened that ordinarily would have spooked Nat, but since his involvement with GodGod, he had come to accept the unimaginable as normal. Not only did Nat hear what the speaker was saying, but he "heard" what the speaker was thinking. With this newfound ability, Nat could discern whether someone was telling the truth, bending it, or just flat-out lying. He concluded, after hearing all the leaders make their cases, that the majority were bald-faced liars.

Nat had a controllable urge to shout out his conclusion, but knew that if he did he would be booted out. So instead of giving voice to his revelation, he stared at each leader and, without moving his lips, mouthed their name and added, "Liar, liar, pants on fire!" In the midst of mouthing, "pants on fire," a blinding flash of the brightest of white lights flashed from the television screens and shone down on him. He shouted, "Yeow!" and threw up his hand to shield his eyes from the glare.

Paul Bluett had described just such a blinding shaft of white light shining down on him when he commandeered the taxi. Nat's head was spinning, and he might have blacked out had he not heard a voice call out, "Yes, you, sir, in the last row of the press section, what is your question?"

While Nat had been focused on "hearing" the world leader's inner thoughts, he had missed hearing the Chairman announce, "The floor is now open for questions."

"Sir," the Chairman repeated loudly, "what is your question?"

"My question?" Nat asked into the microphone an usher offered him.

"Yes," the chairman nodded. "You called out 'Yeow' and raised your hand."

Nat, realizing that the hand he had raised to shield his eyes was still up, answered, "Yes, sir. I did raise my hand."

"Then, sir," Chairman Nahari continued, "please state your name and affiliation!"

"Nat Noland, *New York Times*!" he announced proudly and defiantly, as if daring Krugman or Dowd to challenge him.

Nat knew that this was it! This was his opportunity to start the building of a brave new world.

"And to whom, Mister Noland," the Chairman asked, "do you wish to address your question?"

"If I may, Mr. Chairman, I would like to address my question to the world leaders who this afternoon spoke so eloquently on the subject of war. I have but one question, which our distinguished guests may answer by simply raising their hands."

"You make a reasonable request, Mr. Noland, and, I might add, an expedient one. So, Ladies and Gentlemen, if there are no objections?"

The good-natured buzz that ensued contained an equal proportion of tacit approval and reluctant acquiescence—topped off by nervous laughter when the former President of the United States quipped, "Fire away, Noland!"

Nat was not quite sure how he was going to frame his question, but he knew that the criterion was for it to elicit an answer that would obviously be a truthful one.

As Nat started to formulate his question, he stopped and cocked his head. His newly developed inner ear was receiving an informative e-mail from GodGod. Nat was no longer surprised by the inexplicable and accepted this new e-mail–reception technology. With confidence in his handlers, Nat passed their information on.

"Distinguished Heads of State," Nat began, "before I ask my question, I call your attention to the screens that flank the podium. Two events of uncommon interest recently occurred in our city, and the events were recorded on cell phones by eye witnesses."

Nat took a deep breath and called out, "Roll the tape!" Miraculously, the assembled heads of state and countless millions of viewers throughout the world saw the proscribed punishments meted out to a man who acted selfishly and to a father who mistreated his child.

The viewing of Paul Bluett ungainly hopping up and down on a street corner drew sporadic laughter peppered with whispered comments doubting the tapes' authenticity or value.

"It's a hoax!"

"Why are we watching this silliness?"

"What misguided idiot sanctioned this screening?"

Paul Bluett's high-hopping received a fair amount of laughter, but when the man with the face full of pus-festering boils made his appearance, the laughter subsided, and the sounds of retching and vomiting filled the hall—then the screen went black.

A moment later it lit up and projected on it was a close-up of the last man in the world Nat expected to see—Paul Bluett! Over the sound of the sickened audience reacting to the boil-stricken father, Paul calmly identified himself as both "the author of the daily column 'Think About This' and the unwilling star of the hopping-man sequence you all seemed to enjoy so much."

Even more unexpected for Nat was hearing his friend tell the world that his hopping affliction and the mean father's breaking out in boils had actually occurred and were deserved punishments. This from a man who only hours ago had insisted that

he did not want his wife or his readers—or anyone—
to know about his humiliating experience.

The biggest, mind-blowing surprise was yet
to come, and Nat was not ready to process it.
Following Paul's image on the giant screens was that
of a man who identified himself as an eyewitness to
the pus-oozing punishment of the monster who
battered his young son. Although Nat did not
recognize the man, there was something in the
timbre of his voice that was eerily familiar. When Nat
heard the man identify himself, he could barely
restrain himself from shouting, "Holy shit!"

"My name is Rhyne Karlner," the man
announced, "and I was not a witness to that man's
cruelty, but a young girl was, and she recorded what
you saw and gave the tape to me. I came upon the
scene just as the father ran off screaming in pain. I
also saw someone lying on the ground. It was a man
who I later learned was Nat Noland. He had
obviously viewed the scene and had done what most
of us would have…blacked out. He can fill you in on
the horrible details. By the way, he may be too
modest to admit it, but it was Mr. Noland who had
written a letter to God suggesting how—if good
deeds would be immediately rewarded and bad deeds
immediately punished—our world would be a better

place. I am here simply to lend my support to what Mr. Noland has undertaken and suggest that you do likewise. Thank you."

The stunned audience, which up to now had remained passive and decorous, suddenly turned into an angry mob. To a man and woman, they stood up and railed at the Chairman, demanding that he apologize for preempting an important event to insult and disgust the honored guests of the United Nations. At the height of their shouted invectives, flashing down from the giant screens, was an even brighter white light than the one that had shone down on Nat earlier, and the pulsating halation that now enveloped him brought immediate decorum back into the hall.

From all that had transpired, Nat knew that he had no choice but to give in to the immutable forces he was responsible for setting in motion. He raised the microphone to his lips and spoke:

"I never expected to be here at the United Nations addressing our distinguished world leaders just because I offered God a few suggestions, but here I am. Before showing you the 'Just Desserts' two people were given for their behavior, I had been about to ask a question that can be responded to by a raising of hands. I think it is only fair to warn you that one of my suggestions to God was for Him to punish leaders whose lies and deceits inflict physical and emotional pain on their people. It would be remiss of me not to remind you that the God who visited the punishments on the two people you viewed on the screens will mete out appropriately stricter punishments to those who lied about sending people to kill and die in unnecessary wars."

Nat paused to scan the sea of suspicious, unfriendly faces glaring up at him.

"In keeping with the subject on which you have all spoken so eloquently, my question is this: Did you, when deciding to take your country to war, do so to protect your personal best interests and the financial interests of giant corporations friendly to you and your political party? Raise your hand if you acted in this fashion."

For a discomforting length of time no one spoke, no one moved, and no one breathed. The wind that had been blowing off the East River suddenly stopped, and the national flags gracing the entrance outside the great hall went limp, as did the spines and genitalia of their world leaders inside the hall.

"Perhaps my question was ambiguous...?" Nat suggested to the non-committal leaders, "...so allow me to rephrase it. I must warn you, however, that whether or not you raise your hand, we will know if your answer is truthful."

Nat thought for a moment, then in a loud clear voice stated:

"The motivating reason I took my country to war was to protect the lives of our citizens and the moral integrity of our nation. If this is true, please raise your hand."

This time, without hesitation, all but one leader raised their hands.

Nat had no idea what GodGod had in mind as punishment for the liars and expected that something would happen, but nothing did. He thought, "Was it possible that all had honestly taken their country to war for moral reasons?" That would seem to be the case.

Nat was confused as he watched the leaders nod to one another and look in smug suspicion at the one who did not raise his hand.

"Mr. Noland, we thank you for your insightful question," Chairman Nahari commented from the podium, "and we thank our distinguished guests for their candor. It is heartening to know that the overwhelming majority of our world leaders…"

The chairman was interrupted by the sound of quiet sniffling coming from somewhere in the hall. The sniffling persisted, and all eyes turned to watch a small array of white handkerchiefs being retrieved by those who had just responded to Nat's question.

"Sniffles?" Nat thought. "This is their just punishment for lying about why they took their country to war? *A bout of the sniffles?*"

Just as Nat was thinking "sniffles," a major sneezing fit overtook the snifflers. After a dozen consecutive brain-rattling sneezes, the leaders of state, as if given the military order, "Blow noses, blow!" simultaneously blew their noses. The volume was so ear shatteringly loud and the reverberating noise so powerful that one would have thought it was the result of a thousand noses being blown—not a mere seven.

Immediately after the nasal explosion, each leader of state, as if choreographed, pulled the hanky from his nose and looked to see the result of his giant "bloozer." All showed disappointment and confusion and looked again. On the screen, the world saw an expanse of white cloth with no nasal residue. Again, as if programmed, the leaders of state wiggled their noses, neatly folded their hankies, and pocketed them. Then, with quizzical looks on their faces, each scratched or rubbed his nose and looked across to check what was happening to a fellow member. Soon they all gathered around the former President of the United States who was alternately wiggling, scratching, and rubbing his nose harder than most.

They all watched as he retrieved his handkerchief and blew hard into it, the sound rivaling the one made by the group a few moments before. This time he did not pull the hanky from his nose to look at what he had blown out of it, but instead held it there for a few moments and then touched it lightly with his fingertips. With panic starting to mount, he looked to his nearest trusted ally, the Prime Minister of England, and beckoned to him.

"Fred," he asked, moving his hanky to one side, "is there something growing on my nose?"

"No, there's nothing growing on your nose, but," the Prime Minister said softly, "I never realized it was so prominent."

"It is not prominent!" the former President barked. "My nose is my most complimented feature. Cartoonists have always had difficultly ridiculing it."

"That may change," the Prime Minister countered, "if your nose continues to become any more prominent."

"Someone hand me a mirror!" the former President shouted to an aide.

He then held one hand over his nose and pointedly said to the Prime Minister, "Before you start casting stones, Freddy-boy, check your own nose!"

On the giant screen it was there for all to see. Not only were the former President's and the Prime Minister's noses starting to grow longer but so were the noses of all the other leaders of state—except the Prime Minister of Spain, who, by not raising his hand, admitted that he took his country to war for other than moral reasons. His nose, although it did not grow longer like the others continued to do, became red-veined and bulbous.

"What hath I wrought?" Nat wondered. "And what hath GodGod in mind when he devised this Pinocchio-inspired punishment?"

What GodGod had in mind became clearer and clearer as the leaders' noses grew longer and longer. The seven who were afflicted found themselves turning to look at each other, and when they did their foot-long noses bumped each other's arms or shoulders or cheeks. They found themselves stepping back and forming a circle where, as their noses grew, each took on the appearance of being a spoke in the "Wheel of *Mis*fortune."

What followed was of personal interest to everyone in the great hall, and so that all could see clearly the details of the unfolding saga, the growing noses were projected onto the two giant screens. Nat assumed correctly that this was courtesy of Rhyne Karlner and his "spirited" crew.

The madness that was transpiring at The United Nations was being seen in every country in the world by every citizen old enough to know or understand the difference between the truth and a lie, between moral and amoral, selflessness and selfishness, and what may happen to people who refuse to learn right from wrong.

Completely mesmerized by the unfolding drama, Nat was jolted when he heard his name filtering through the cacophony:

"Mr. Noland, Mr. Noland, Mister Nat Noland!" blared Chairman Nahari's voice. "Assembled guests, for sanity's sake, I beg you to please be quiet! It is imperative that I speak with Mr. Noland! Mr. Noland?"

Miraculously, as if a master switch were thrown, all heeded the chairman's plea, and the hall became graveyard quiet. The only audible sound heard under the Chairman's voice was the soft whimpering of the world's leaders as they watched their noses slowly grow longer and longer.

"Mr. Noland," the Chairman pleaded, "it was your question that evoked this...this growth phenomenon. I trust you know of a method to reverse it?"

Nat, completely nonplussed and ill-equipped to answer, looked blankly to where the hysterical dignitaries were dealing badly with their problem—one official with two hands on his nose looked as if he were playing a clarinet. Nat wanted to laugh but instead prayed that GodGod would intervene and show him the way.

"Mr. Noland," the Chairman shouted, "I asked if you knew of an available antidote for this!"

Not wanting to be the bearer of horrible tidings, Nat nodded his head and shouted, "Antidote? Yes, sir, there is an antidote…but…but…"

"I don't want 'buts,' Mr. Noland. I want action!" the Chairman screamed. "As your Chairman I am issuing you an executive order! Get that goddamned antidote down here right now!"

CHAPTER 17

As he stood frozen in the press box, Nat considered his options. He could obey the chairman's executive order and pretend to be bringing the antidote to him, or he could jump off the balcony and kill himself—or he could pray that one of his stalwart handlers had a miraculous plan to extricate him from all this.

"Now, Noland," the Chairman bellowed, "NOW! AND THAT'S AN ORDER!"

Nat started to leave the press box but stopped when he heard another voice shout, "NOLAND STAY WHERE YOU ARE!"

It was the voice of Rhyne Karlner, whose image now filled the giant screens.

"Mr. Chairman, Nat Noland does not have the antidote," Rhyne Karlner stated, "but if anyone whose nose is growing wishes to have it in order to stop the process, I suggest you hear me out."

Nat leaned forward in his seat, as did the leaders whose long noses were slowly adding millimeters.

"Firstly," Rhyne began, "I must warn everyone watching that what you saw happen to these gentlemen can happen to you. So if you wish to avoid their predicament, pay attention to my words!"

There had never been a more rapt audience than the one made up of the seven afflicted leaders and their hypnotized onlookers.

Rhyne Karlner smiled benignly as he held up a Bible-size, leather-bound book which bore the title *You Will Know* and the subtitle *Just Desserts*.

"*You Will Know?*" Nat exploded. "That was the first e-mail I received from GodGod!... And *Just Desserts* is the alternate title I'm considering for *Blurbs*! This is too much!"

With the mélange of moaning, wailing, keening, and cursing spewing from the seven leaders, Nat's outburst went unnoticed by everyone except Rhyne Karlner, who glanced toward the press box and winked—a wink that signaled to Nat that his contribution to this historical event was being recognized. Nat could not fully comprehend or process the treasure trove of extraordinary material he was accumulating for his book but knew he would put it to great use. At the moment, Nat was riveted on Rhyne Karlner, who raised his arm and immediately the wailing, keening, and cursing cut off abruptly as if reacting to a conductor's baton.

"The information I am about to give you is written in this good book, *You Will Know*," Rhyne said, holding it up. "Read it and *you will know* how and why to make good decisions in your personal and political lives, and *you will know* why good and bad things happen to people."

"Get on with it, Karlner," an impatient voice demanded. "Tell me how to stop my nose from growing!"

"It states here," Rhyne said, reading from his book, "that those of you who wish to stop their noses from growing may do so by simply raising your hand…if…!"

Before Rhyne could finish his sentence, all seven of the world leaders shot their hands into the air. To their utter dismay, their noses continued to grow and so did their anger. In four languages the leaders of state screamed the equivalent of, "My nose is still growing, you lying, despicable bastard!"

"Yes, your noses are still growing," Rhyne shot back, "because you raised your hands before I finished the instructions. Now put your hands down and listen.

"I repeat: If you wish to stop your nose from growing, raise your hand if…IF…," Rhyne said loudly, "if you admit you lied about something that affected the lives and well being of others."

Rhyne looked from one leader to another and explained as if talking to children, "For instance, if you lied about the reasons you took your country to war, raise your hand and your nose will stop growing."

All eyes focused on the seven leaders of state—their noses were now well over two-feet long. They all stood frozen save for the Prime Minister of Spain whose hand shot up into the air. Miraculously his bulbous nose returned to normal, and he shouted out a heartfelt, "Gracias Dios, gracias!"

Within seconds all whose noses were now approaching the three-foot mark raised their hands high and waved them wildly, and, as promised, their noses stopped growing.

CHAPTER 18

Glennie was worried sick. It had been forty-eight hours since The United Nations had ended its historic session and her husband had contacted her on his dying cell phone. Their static-laden exchange was short, confused, and frustrating.

"Nat, I saw you on television…you were…"

"It wasn't me…it wasn't me," Nat whined, his head pounding.

"It sure looked like you. Nat, are you coming home?"

"As soon as I can put the pieces together!" he said, pressing his thumb to his right temple.

"What pieces, Nat?"

"All the goddamned pieces that make me, me!" he shouted, then dropped his cell phone and blacked out.

Dozens of people passed the motionless body that lay in a heap, thinking that it was a wretched homeless person trying to make a social statement by sleeping on the cold marble in front of the U.N. If it were not for an empathetic woman delegate from Darfur, who took the time to notice that the "homeless" man needed medical attention, it might have been hours before Nat was admitted to the emergency room at Mount Sinai. Unfortunately, moments before the Good Samaritan called the paramedics, a deft pickpocket had lifted Nat's press pass and wallet—so he was registered as John Doe.

While the doctors were trying to determine whether or not John Doe was asleep or in a coma (the consensus: "a mentally provoked, hypnotic sleep-coma"), John Doe and the attending staff were unaware of the exalted status of Nat Noland.

They had no idea that the network and cable stations were camped in the street below his windows, waiting to capture candid photos of the man being called, "The Twenty-First Century's Grandest Inquisitor!"

John Doe was not aware that it was Paul Bluett who had dubbed him that in his column, and now every radio, television, and print source throughout the world was referring to novelist Nat Noland as "The Grandest Inquisitor."

The one thing John Doe was not privy to and would have enjoyed knowing was the fate of the extremely long-nosed world leaders. His heart would be singing to know that two resigned, three had been impeached, and two fled to the Cayman Islands, where they were unwelcomed and returned to face jail sentences.

John Doe reclaimed his identity a few days later when one of the more perceptive nurses noticed how much the unshaven John Doe resembled Nat Noland, The Grandest Inquisitor, who was peering at her from the television screen.

The following day, Nat was delivered to his home where Glennie and the girls, assisted by a crack staff of medical personnel, kept a loving and constant vigil waiting for him to awaken. That same night, Glennie lay down next to her husband and wrapped his limp arms around her waist, hoping to approximate their normal sleeping mode. Glennie fell asleep holding his arms in place about her and awoke to hear Nat's voice, speaking quietly but saying— what she described later as "the sweetest, dearest, most wonderful words she ever heard"—"Darling, I have to pee...."

CHAPTER 19

R oss Davidoff read the final page of Nat Noland's new novellelah, smiled and shook his head. It was a first for the distinguished publisher. Never before had he agreed to read an author's work the moment it was handed to him, and never, ever, could he imagine reading it while the author napped on his couch not ten feet from him.

The quiet sigh that escaped Ross Davidoff and the sound of the manuscript being laid down on his desk was loud enough to awaken the anxious author.

"So, Ross," Nat said nervously as he sat up, "I see you finished reading it…I did tell you that it will be a page or so longer, at most. A session or two more with Dr. Frucht, and I'll have what I need to tie up some of the looser ends. By the way, Dr. Frucht has really helped me with this book, but I'm thinking of not using his name. I might call him Dr Friel or Froman…. I'm rattling on, aren't I? I should let you talk. So, what do you think, Ross?"

"To borrow a phrase you put in my mouth on page sixty-eight," Ross said, opening to a page he had dog-eared, "'Nat, I'll get back to you!' I couldn't resist that, Nat," Ross said, laughing as he hefted the manuscript, "but seriously, about this…"

"Pretty nutty book, huh?" Nat asked, anticipating a rejection.

"Yes, it is, as you say, a pretty nutty book—it is also quite original."

"…and damned entertaining, won't you admit?" Nat urged.

"Okay, Nat, I'll admit, damned entertaining, but…?

"No, you cannot have a 'but,'" Nat bellowed dramatically.

"I do," Ross insisted. "I have a big 'but'…"

"Big enough to counter 'pretty nutty, quite original, and damned entertaining'? You can't have a 'butt' that big! Is it about ending the book with my saying, 'I have to pee'?"

"No, that was sort of cute."

"I thought it was…but I don't end the book with that. Ross, are you concerned about my using real names?"

"Actually, that is one of my…"

"It's done. I worried it might make problems for Dr. Frucht, although he didn't ask me to change it."

"I don't have an opinion about Dr. Frucht," Ross offered cautiously, "but I do feel that you should give serious thought to changing…"

"What? Changing what?" Nat challenged, ready to defend his turf.

"Well, like changing the name of your central character."

"What are you saying? I shouldn't use my own name?"

"Yes. Your readers will know that some of the events in the book did not happen to Nat Noland."

"But most of them did, Ross!"

"*Most?*"

"Well, a lot!"

"A lot?"

"A good twenty percent!"

"Nat, twenty percent is not a lot."

"It's a hundred percent more than nothing! What you don't understand, Ross, is that I am not only Nat Noland, I am everyone in this damn book! Everyone but you, my wife Glennie, and the celebrities, Larry Gelbart, Mel Brooks, Philip Roth or Richard Dawkins who, if you recall, gave my book raves, but it was *me* who did the raving!"

Ross was itching to say, "Because you are a raving lunatic," but said instead, "Be that as it may,

but you, Nat Noland, are just too well known...
you've been on every talk show. Your readers
know you!"

"And they trust me!" Nat said, putting his
face close to Ross. "In my last book, I wrote about
my discovering that I was a quadruplet and
searching out and reuniting with my three siblings,
and they believed me because it was true!"

"And was proven to be true because there
were photos of you and your brothers printed in all
the newspapers," Ross argued. "There are no photos
of Nat Noland addressing the U.N. and no
newspaper headlines proclaiming you to be the
'Twenty-First Century's Grandest Inquisitor.'"

"Not yet there isn't...but who's to say that by
the year 2010 there won't be," Nat said, brandishing
the manuscript. "Ross, this nutty, quite original,
darned entertaining book could also turn out to be
darned prophetic!"

"Aha!" Ross pounced. "That was my 'but'..."

"You don't think it can be prophetic?" Nat
challenged.

"It may or it may not be. The bottom line is
book sales...immediate and future book sales! What
I am saying is I want our company to publish
Blurbs."

"*Just Desserts*.... I may change it to *Just Desserts*. I'm sorry, Ross, you were saying?"

"I was saying that you would be doing us and yourself a service if, instead of setting your novel in the year 2010, you change it to 2015. In that way..."

"...in that way," Nat said, excitedly taking the baton, "I will have five years before I am proven to be prophetic or full of crap!"

"Which translates into five added years of book sales for our company...and for you, Mister Noland."

"It worked for George Orwell's *1984*," Nat laughed. "His warning about a complete totalitarian society is still a possibility. We may never learn whether or not he's full of crap."

CHAPTER 20

K nowing that he was nearing the finish line, Nat Noland started smiling the moment he woke up this morning and could not stop. He smiled as he booted up his computer and looked at the right corner of the screen and saw looking back at him: page number 133! If all went well in the next day or so, he will have completed a credible and not too shabby novellelah. He closed his eyes, checked the back of his eyelids for a possible last inspiration, and there it was—in bold face—**QUOTE**.

He thought, "It might be nice to have one more quote to add to my distinguished list. This time I ought to try to get a bona fide blurb from a willing celebrity, one who will write something positive and mean it…but who? Do I know such a person?"

No sooner than he had posed that question, he had the answer. Three years ago he had met a friendly author-director-actor at a literary luncheon, and they had exchanged novels and e-mailed each other flattering compliments.

"Why not?" he thought and sent off his manuscript along with his e-mail address and a note,

"I would be honored to have a quote, if you feel that *Just Desserts* deserves a positive one."

Two days later, Nat was surprised and delighted to receive the following e-mail:

> *Dear Nat,*
>
> *Thank you for sending* Just Desserts. *Had a good time reading it, and here is my "positive" opinion to do with what you will: "After reading the last page of Nat Noland's* Just Desserts, *I thought, 'Now, here is a book I would be proud to have written.'"*
>
> *Carl Reiner*

Nat immediately added this to the Gelbart, Brooks, Roth, and Dawkins quotes and smiled. The Reiner quote was honest, bona fide and positive, but somehow it lacked the depth, wit, and persuasive power of the ones he had written for the more important and better-known celebrities. Nat decided not to include the Reiner blurb on the jacket—and not to send him a signed advance copy of the book.

Nat again checked the page count of his novelellah and sighed, "Hm, one hundred and thirty four pages…oops, okay so it's a novellelah plus…a little less pithy than I had planned, but pithy enough."

ADDENDELLAH

N at could not sleep. His book was put to bed, but his brain would not allow itself the luxury of lying down and taking a nap. To lull himself to sleep he decided to see how many distinguished-sounding names he could invent— names that might be found on book reviews in small city newspapers. Nat brought up a blank screen and created these little known but highly respected academicians:

> *Professor Ashleigh Banista*
> *Geoffrey D. Hoblein*
> *Dr. Garth James, Sr.*
> *Emanuel Pabst III*
> *Gunther Ross-Keebler*
> *Mme. Martha Couric*
> *W. Benjamin Geisler*
> *Dr. Millicent Saint-Hubbins*

Nat stopped when he had typed forty scholarly-sounding candidates from which to choose. One third he designated as PhDs, and one he awarded a Nobel Prize. Perhaps these erudite phantoms will, one day, write excellent reviews of *Just Desserts*—reviews that Nat would be more than happy to ghostwrite for them.